All Our Yesterdays

By Guy Hale

Act II in the Shakespeare Murders series

A Bullington Press publication
Copyright © Guy Hale, 2025

ISBN 978-1-0683633-2-0 (paperback)
ISBN 978-1-0683633-4-4 (e-book)
ISBN 978-1-0683633-6-8 (special edition hardback)

For permission requests, please email: info@bullingtonpress.co.uk

Interior layout by Textual Eyes
Design for Print Services

Cover painting by Amy Newport
Cover design by Peter Adlington

Printed and bound by CPI Group (UK) Ltd, Croydon, CR0 4YY

www.bullingtonpress.co.uk

A Novella Prequel to The Croaking Raven set in pre-war, golden age theatre land. Giant egos, shocking secrets, devilish scheming and backstabbing.

Paul Burke (Crime Time FM)

Praise for the Shakespeare Murder series

Absolutely superb. I loved the darkness of it.

Chris Lloyd (winner of the HWA Gold Crown)

Deeply satisfying, great writing. A dark tale and a cracking read.

David Penny (author of The Thomas Berrington Historical Mysteries)

Dark, twisted and hilarious. Hale's characters are so well drawn. A brilliant read. Get thee to a bookshop.

Heather Critchlow (author of the Cal Lovett Series)

Superb writing, a masterpiece. Crime, Shakespeare and humour. What more could you ask from a book?

Aimee Louise (@whataimeereads_)

This was a book I fell in love with from the opening pages and was totally hooked right up to the unexpected ending. Can't wait for the next in this highly original series.

Andy Wormald (@amwbooks)

Wildly entertaining, darkly funny. Hamlet as you've never seen it. Had me gripped and gasping. Outstanding!

Rob Parker (author of the Thirty Miles Trilogy)

Dexter meets Shakespeare in this dark and twisted tale of revenge.

Christie J. Newport (Joffe Books prize winner)

Masterful plotting, a dark and funny take on Hamlet.

Blair Kessler (The Birmingham Film Company)

I loved this book. Very atmospheric. This Hamlet is extremely good but also very bad!

Imran Mahmood (author of I Know What I Saw)

Fresh, funny and fiendishly clever. The Croaking Raven is an absolute triumph!

A.A. Chaudhuri (Amazon bestselling author)

By Guy Hale

The Comeback Trail Trilogy

Killing Me Softly
Blood on the Tracks
All the World's a Stage

The Shakespeare Murders

The Croaking Raven
All Our Yesterdays

For Blair and Lynn Kessler

Two wonderful friends
I inherited from my parents
fifty years ago.

All Our Yesterdays

The Journal of
Felix Richards

Prologue

Memories are poor historians, coloured as they are by emotion, love, regret and a hundred different thoughts of what was and what could have been. This is not a historical document but a memoir about people I loved, some more than others.

It was the spring of 1932 and everything seemed possible. The ravages of the great depression had hit us all. Work was hard to find and industry had withered like the fruit of a poisoned vine. Little did we know that, soon, the silent factories would spring back to life, powered by a need for the weapons of death. War, always good for business but little else, would put the nation back to work, but that was seven years away and we were in Stratford-upon-Avon.

I was a young actor and my friend, Morris Oxford, had landed the lead role in Julius Caesar. It was the first season at the new Shakespeare Memorial Theatre after the terrible fire of 1926 had burned the old one to the ground. This would be a prestigious season. Morris, already regarded as potentially one of the greats of the stage, had started his own company. I was lucky enough to be part of that company and would play Mark Antony.

It was a huge responsibility but Morris wore the pressure lightly, self-doubt had never been an issue for him. That was where the seeds of his greatness were sown, the point at which he took control of his own destiny and of those around him. I see it now, of course, time lends perspective, but then? No. I was young, starstruck. Happy to be a mere satellite in orbit around him. I was born in Hollywood. No, not that one. Hollywood, to the south of Birmingham, a journey of just eighteen miles but a lifetime away from the rarefied atmosphere of Shakespeare's Stratford.

This was where it all began, where the seeds were sown. Some would grow to greatness and others … Well, that's a tale to be told. We were gathered as a company, drawn from all over the country, the brightest and the best. These were happy times and the possibilities of our youth seemed endless. We should have known.

Shakespeare was the master of comedies but his greatest plays were tragedies and we, unwittingly, were trapped in one of our own. But all our yesterdays have lighted fools the way to dusty death. The play had begun and we were but players.

The story that lay before us was unknown. Life, like a hand of cards, has its aces and jokers. It's a journey we undertake without ever knowing the route we will follow; time and circumstance will dictate. The only thing we ever know is the destination. There is no guarantee of any man living through the seven ages. Some, as you will discover, did not. We didn't know that then, how could we? All any of us knew for certain is that, at some unappointed hour, the clock would strike and the bell would sound its toll. When it did, best not ask for whom the bell tolls, it could toll for thee. I shall leave it to the Bard to sum up the course of a human life; no one ever did it better.

All the world's a stage,
And all the men and women merely players;
They have their exits and their entrances,
And one man in his time plays many parts,
His acts being seven ages. At first the infant,
Mewling and puking in the nurse's arms.
Then, the whining schoolboy with his satchel
And shining morning face, creeping like snail
Unwillingly to school. And then the lover,
Sighing like furnace, with a woeful ballad
Made to his mistress' eyebrow. Then, a soldier,
Full of strange oaths, and bearded like the pard,
Jealous in honour, sudden, and quick in quarrel,

Seeking the bubble reputation
Even in the cannon's mouth. And then, the justice,
In fair round belly, with a good capon lined,
With eyes severe, and beard of formal cut,
Full of wise saws, and modern instances,
And so he plays his part. The sixth age shifts
Into the lean and slipper'd pantaloon,
With spectacles on nose and pouch on side,
His youthful hose, well saved, a world too wide
For his shrunk shank, and his big manly voice,
Turning again toward childish treble, pipes
And whistles in his sound. Last scene of all,
That ends this strange eventful history,
Is second childishness and mere oblivion,
Sans teeth, sans eyes, sans taste, sans everything.

Chapter 1
Veni, Vidi, Vici (I Came, I Saw, I Conquered)

When Morris Oxford entered a room, everyone noticed. Even the sound of his footsteps had gravitas. When he spoke, his voice echoed and we were in awe – with one exception, but more on Richard Jenkins later. Morris looked at our troupe – *his* company of actors – smiled, and then addressed us.

'I just wanted to say a few words before tonight's performance. It's a full house and there is huge expectation of us. We have rehearsed well, we know our entrances and our exits. We understand the text, all we have to do is repeat what we have perfected in rehearsal in front of a live audience. That is all. Do that and greatness beckons.'

There was laughter from the back of the room; it was Richard. 'It's only a play, man.'

All heads turned to look at the smiling Welshman and then back to Morris.

'No, Richard, it's THE play. The one we are performing tonight and thus the only play that matters in our world at this moment. The eyes of the press will be upon us. We must succeed.'

Richard nodded. 'OK, Morris, I'm sure it'll be fine.'

Morris stared at Richard for several seconds, his face a mask. Undecided which expression to wear, he smiled. 'Thanks, Richard. I may have slightly overstated the gravity of the situation, but this is the company's first performance and I want it to be good. Hell, I want it to be great.'

'It will be,' cried Desmond Tharpe in his best role of arse-licker-in-chief. 'With you as our leader, how could it fail?' He started to clap and the rest of the cast joined in, even Richard.

And so it began, the career of Morris Oxford. A career that would lead to a knighthood, world-wide acclaim and marriage to the wife of Richard Jenkins. We didn't know it then but our happy little band would soon have tragedy and death visited upon us. Youth is often blind to the harsh realities of life; success is a mountain, with more than one path to the top.

The performance that night was indeed a triumph. Morris was a brilliant Caesar and received huge applause for his performance. It should have been a great moment for him but, from where I stood on the stage, I could see a slight discomfort to his demeanour.

In contrast, I had not acted with Richard before and, therefore, was taken aback by the disarming emotion of his performance. He embodied the conflict that was tearing Brutus apart. Caesar was his friend and yet he had orchestrated his murder. He was an honourable man, torn between the love of his friend and his duty to the Roman Empire. It was a tour de force, all emotion laid bare.

During my scenes with him, I was mesmerised by his intensity and had to concentrate to avoid falling into an open-mouthed stare. I was in awe of his talent. Nobody in the theatre that night could have missed it, and they didn't. When Richard took his applause, the roof nearly lifted off the theatre as cheers rang out. He took it calmly, without show, and then backed away to allow Morris to take his applause which, while rapturous, was not as loud or enthusiastic as Richard's.

Most wouldn't have noticed, but I did. When I looked across at Morris, he was glaring at Richard – a forced smile glued to his face. This was the beginning of the tragedy of Richard Jenkins and all those that were part of that company. The fingers of that tragedy would reach out over time and touch the lives of many: Beatrice Smallman, the beautiful young actress who had played

Portia and was married to Richard. Oliver, who, at that moment, was growing silently in her womb and would one day become the seed of their destruction. Ambition when uncontained can be a fatal flaw.

When we returned to the dressing room, we were elated. The audience's applause still rang in our ears.

'Who fancies celebrating properly?'

I turned to Richard. 'What're you thinking?'

'Dirty Duck, of course.'

There was a cheer from the cast and the dressing room emptied rapidly as everyone headed for the pub. I was about to follow when I noticed Morris sitting alone in the corner of the room. His make-up was untouched and he looked into his mirror as if at a stranger.

'You coming, Morris?'

He didn't acknowledge me, lost in his own reflection, seeing something that only he could.

I walked over to him and put my hand on his shoulder. 'You coming, Morris?'

He didn't turn but his eyes found mine in the mirror. 'You saw it, didn't you?'

'Saw what?'

'Richard.'

'Oh, that.'

'Yes, that, how did he do that?'

I shrugged. 'I don't know. Just a good actor, I guess.'

Morris shook his head. 'It's more than that, Felix. I played the role of Caesar tonight but he *was* Brutus! I felt his pain, saw the conflict in his eyes as he betrayed me. That wasn't acting, that was something else. I don't think I can do that.' There was despair in his voice.

He was acknowledging what I already knew; he wasn't the greatest actor of his generation, he wasn't even the best actor in his own company. Richard had shown him what was possible and he had no comprehension of how to match him.

'Cheer up, Morris. It's your name over the door and Richard works for you. Any glory he gets will reflect on you.'

'Yes. It will, won't it.' Morris wiped the make-up from his face. 'I decide who plays each role. His brilliance can be contained. Let's get to the Dirty Duck.'

It was a chilling statement. It didn't register at the time but, looking back, it was a clear signal of intent. Morris had realised that he could not match what Richard had, but he could prevent him from showing it. Give him the lesser roles. Rob him of stage time and the opportunity to display that awesome talent. He looked in the mirror and smiled at me.

'Veni, vidi, vici,' he proclaimed. 'I came, I saw, I conquered.' We both laughed.

Little did I realise just how serious Morris was, and that this ovation would be the highlight of Richard's career.

Chapter 2
Fault Lines

After the run of Julius Caesar, the world of stage was Morris Oxford's oyster. He was the heir apparent to the throne. His only problem? The throne he sought was occupied.

Sir Miles Tennyson was the great Shakespearian actor of the day. He had bestridden the stage like a colossus for nearly forty years. He was much loved in Stratford, and Morris didn't like it. Although he played public lip service to Sir Miles' greatness, behind the scenes, he didn't hold back.

'Have you read this crap?' Morris offered me The Guardian he was reading.

I took it from him; it was a review of Sir Miles' performance in King Lear. 'What's it say?'

'Nothing, just the usual fawning adoration. The man just has to walk on stage and he gets an ovation.'

'Well, that could be you one day, Morris. All you have to do is wait your turn.'

'But I don't want to wait, Felix. I'm better than him.'

There wasn't much I could say to that. Sir Miles was loved by generations of theatregoers that had grown up watching him. His talent was adequate, but he was nowhere near the level of Morris. Even so, nostalgia is a strong emotion.

'It's dead man's shoes syndrome, you're just going to have to wait until he retires or dies,' I said.

Morris scowled. 'He'll only retire when he dies, I've seen his like before. Preserved in claret and unkillable. He could go on for another twenty years.'

'Cheer up, Morris. You're barely thirty, the world's your oyster. Be patient and the world will come to you.'

Morris fixed me with a stare I will never forget; in that look I saw the desire, the *need* to be acknowledged as the greatest. Raw, unfettered ambition. It was uncomfortable to behold.

'Dead man's shoes, you say.'

I nodded and he shook his head. 'What if I can't wait that long?'

I had thought we were alone but, as I turned to leave, I noticed Beatrice Smallman standing in the doorway. In her arms, she held her newborn son.

'Beatrice, how wonderful.' I went over to her and gazed into the eyes of young Oliver. 'He's a beautiful boy.'

Beatrice smiled. 'Takes after his dad.'

'And his mother,' said Morris. The sight of Beatrice cradling Oliver seemed to have lightened his mood and now he was all smiles. He patted Beatrice on the back. 'Well done, Beatie, well done.'

As he pecked her on the cheek, his hand ran down her back and gently stroked her bottom; I pretended not to see and Beatrice didn't seem to notice. They looked at each other and it was almost as if I wasn't there. I made my excuses and left. Morris was thirty and Beatrice had just turned nineteen. He should have been like a big brother to her, but the look that had passed between them said so much more. To quote Hamlet, something was rotten in the state of Denmark.

The first season at Stratford had gone really well and we were all back the next season to undertake three plays, the first of which was *Hamlet*. It was a given that Morris would be Hamlet; Desmond Tharpe, Polonius; with Beatrice playing his daughter, Ophelia. All the casting made sense until it came to Richard. Would he be Claudius? He could have played that lustful, conniving king with ease but, as Morris read out the cast list, Richard's name was notable for its absence.

After a few moments, Richard could bear it no longer. 'What about me, Morris? Have you forgotten that I'm here?'

'No, of course not, Richard. I would like you to have a go at the Gravedigger.'

'The bloody Gravedigger, are you joking?'

'No, it's a very important scene. Pivotal, in fact.'

None of us knew what to say. It was crazy not to have our best actor in a leading role, but Morris was being true to his word. He had told me he would contain Richard's talent and here was the first example of it. We all fell silent as Richard stood and moved towards Morris.

'The Gravedigger, that's it?'

Morris shrugged. 'You could be Rosencrantz or Guildenstern as well.'

'Do you want me to sell the programmes in the foyer too?'

Morris shook his head. 'No, but I think you could also bring something special to that role.'

Richard clenched his fists. 'I could bring something special to you, Morris.'

Beatrice stepped between them. 'Let's calm it down, Richard. Morris is our leader, I'm sure you'll get a lead in *The Tempest*.' She turned to Morris. 'Won't he?'

Morris gave her a sickly smile. 'Of course, Richard will make an excellent Caliban.' For a moment this seemed to placate Richard, and then Morris added, 'Because he looks like a monster and smells like the sea.'

We all recognised the quote from the play and laughed, except for Richard.

'I'm from the Rhonda Valley not bloody Swansea.'

That was the first of many hostile confrontations between Morris and Richard that season. The happy Camelot Morris had been building was now beginning to crumble. The cracks of resentment were spreading, cracks that would soon open up and swallow Richard whole.

Apart from Morris and Richard, the rest of the company got

on well, we were all young and enthusiastic.

I loved being a full-time actor but had already realised that I wasn't destined for greatness. Acting with Morris and Richard had shown me the standard that was required and I knew I could never reach it, but I was competent and good at comedy. I had found my place, for now.

Desmond Tharpe was also competent but, for someone with even less talent than me, he seemed to get a lot of great roles. In his defence, he always knew his lines and never bumped into the scenery but that was about all. His greatest skill was praising Morris. He took obsequiousness to new levels in his servile obedience to Morris and soon became known as The Spaniel because he always followed Morris around with his tongue out. That said, he was still a likeable chap and we all rubbed happily along, until the first night of *Hamlet*.

Richard had been quietly seething about being ignored for a major role; he had always been an enthusiastic drinker but it had now become habitual. His happy-go-lucky nature had darkened and he seemed to be turning in on himself. Beatrice tried to soothe his anger but she was caught between looking after young Oliver, playing Ophelia and keeping Richard and Morris apart. It was an impossible situation.

Opening night had finally arrived. As I sat in the dressing room, which I shared with Richard and Desmond, I noticed that Richard was smiling. I hadn't seen him do that for weeks.

'Good to see the smile back on your face.'

'Well, I'm looking forward to the show.' His smiled turned to a smirk. 'Can't wait to see how Morris gets on when he has to improvise.'

That didn't sound good. I glanced over at Desmond but he was busy with his eyeliner and clearly hadn't heard the comment.

'You're not going to do anything silly, are you?'

Richard grinned. 'Define silly.'

I knew then that he planned to do something dreadful, but

what? Should I warn Morris without knowing the details?

'Please don't do anything you will regret, Richard.'

He looked at me, a fire of defiance burning in his eyes. 'I have nothing to regret, I'm just a bloody spear-carrier. Morris has seen to that.' He turned back to his mirror and darkened the shadows beneath his eyes. 'Sometimes, spears can be thrown.'

He said it in a whisper but I heard it. A chill ran through me. Richard had planned something and, in the next two hours, I would find out what it was in front of a full house.

The play rolled along, rising and falling to the orchestration of Shakespeare's prose. Like a river flowing to the sea, always gently falling to its ending. It was a fine performance, and then we came to Act 5, Scene 1, affectionately known as 'the Gravedigger scene'. I will never forget it. I was playing Horatio to Morris' Hamlet and so crouched with him watching Richard dig the grave. He had played the comedy well with the other Gravedigger but now came the part where Hamlet spoke to him.

'"Whose grave's this, sirrah?"'

'"Mine, sir."' Richard then sang, as the part required, but with a beautiful voice that rang through the theatre. '"O, a pit of clay for to be made, for such a guest is meet."'

'"I think it be thine indeed, for thou liest in't,"' said Morris.

Richard looked up at him and grinned. 'You know it is mine, for you put me in it.'

This was not the line. I realised at once that this was the revenge Richard had been planning.

Morris barely hesitated and moved to his next line. '"Thou dost lie in't, to be in't and say it is thine. Tis for the dead, not for the quick; therefore, thou liest."'

'"'Tis a quick lie, sir; 'twill away again,"' Richard paused, looked up at Morris and pointed. '"From me to you."' There was threat in his gesture.

Morris continued without pause. '"What man dost thou dig it for?"'

'For you, sir!'

I sensed a stir in the audience from those who knew the play and realised that these were not the words of Shakespeare.

For a split-second, Morris hesitated and then he pushed on, desperately trying to get through the scene. '"What woman then?"'

Richard pointed at Morris again. 'Just for you, sir.'

'"Who is to be buried in't?"' There was an angry insistence to Morris' voice.

'One that was an actor but, rest his soul, he's dead.'

Morris launched into the next speech, showing genuine anger. '"How absolute the knave is!"' He ran through his lines with a venom that was not in the script. '"How long hast thou been grave-maker?"'

'Since you put me in't, sir.'

'"How long is that since?"' demanded Morris, still desperately sticking to the script.

'"Cannot you tell that?"' Richard turned to the audience. '"Every fool can tell that."'

There was a smattering of laughter from the audience but I could also hear a low murmuring. More audience members were sensing that something was amiss on stage.

'"It was that very day that young Hamlet was born."' Richard sprang up from the grave and stood face-to-face with Morris. '"He that is mad, and sent into England."'

Morris was shocked, we all were. Richard had gone completely off script, it was madness. Despite this, his performance was still mesmerising. I feared when it came to my lines, I would be unable to remember them. As these thoughts passed through my mind, I missed several lines.

Morris was still ploughing on, speaking Hamlet's words as if the Gravedigger had been saying his. '"How came he mad?"'

'"Very strangely, they say."'

'"How "strangely"?"'

Richard looked out into the audience. "'Faith, e'en with losing his wits.'"

The audience sniggered.

"'Upon what ground?'" demanded Morris.

'You tell me, mate,' said Richard, departing completely from character. 'I'm just a bloody Gravedigger, you're the artistic director.'

There was a sharp intake of breath from the auditorium as many of the audience realised that a drama unrelated to the play was being enacted on stage. Morris looked at me, his eyes pleading for help.

I saw the skull of Yorick lying in the grave and, in that moment, did the only thing I thought would extricate us from this awful situation. I jumped into the grave, picked up the skull and turned to Morris.

'Do you know this man, Hamlet? Was he not once the King's Jester?'

Morris realised what I had done and took the skull of Yorick from me. "'Alas, poor Yorick. I knew him, Horatio—a fellow of infinite jest, of most excellent fancy.'"

And, with that, we were out of the trap that Richard had set. There were no more lines in that scene for the Gravedigger and the play carried on as if nothing had happened.

But it *had* happened and Morris was in a state of outrage when he stormed into our dressing room after the curtain. 'What the hell was that? You could have ruined the show.' His cheeks were flushed and his face contorted with anger.

Richard simply shrugged. 'Well, if you treat me like a knave, expect me to perform like one.'

'I've never seen anything so unprofessional.'

'Really? Stick around. You ever give me another part like that and I will bury the play without hesitation.'

I could see by Richard's expression that he meant every word.

'Very well, you leave me no choice. You're fired!'

Morris stormed from the room, leaving me and Richard alone.

'You should apologise, Richard. Morris is angry right now, but when he calms down—'

Richard shook his head to silence me. 'Forget it, Felix. I'm done with this company, the great Morris Oxford and his travelling ego. I'd rather do panto than put up with this crap. Besides, I've had an offer.'

'Who from?'

'Bristol Old Vic, *Henry V*.'

It was a hammer blow. Richard was our best actor, perhaps on the verge of greatness. We couldn't afford to lose him.

'You can't be serious. You have a wife and a child here, how could you leave them?'

He turned to me, a look of certainty on his face that would soon be proven wrong. 'Beatrice and Oliver will come with me, of course.'

My heart sank. This company had so much promise and now, in less than a year, it was starting to break up. Richard could see how upset I was and laid a hand upon my shoulder.

'You know I have no future here, Felix. Morris is top dog and he feels threatened by me. There's nothing here for me any more.'

I wanted to argue but knew he was right. With that performance, he had dug his own grave and there was no going back.

Chapter 3
We Happy Few

Word of Richard's sacking quickly spread through the theatre; secrets could never be contained in such a close-knit organisation. A company of actors is an extended family. Crazy aunties, weird uncles and barely contained egos that strut the stage waiting to be discovered, desperate for fame. They are all here, living for the next performance, the next chance to stand upon that stage and feel the electricity from the audience. It's what we live for, the thrill of that moment when the curtain goes up.

The thrill also comes with a downside; get it wrong and the reaction is instant, muted applause followed by crushing reviews from the critics. Being an actor is like walking an emotional tightrope; great until the moment you fall. You are only as good as your last performance and Richard's had been … unusual. Anybody who knew the play would have realised something was very wrong with the Gravedigger scene. The critic from *The Herald* knew his Shakespeare, and his review put another nail in the coffin of Richard's career.

Alas, Poor Richard

For those of us fortunate enough to be there, last night's performance of Hamlet contained new material provided by Richard Jenkins. It clearly came as a surprise to Morris Oxford, who was playing Hamlet. His Hamlet was brilliant, despite having to overcome the ad-libs thrown at him by Jenkins. Clearly, there is a problem within the company, as Jenkins' barbs were aimed squarely at Oxford. Jenkins is a great actor, potentially the greatest of his generation, but this kind of behaviour is unacceptable. Thankfully, Oxford stuck to the script and was saved by Felix Richards who, realising what was happening, jumped into the grave and picked up the skull of Yorick.

"Do you know this man, Hamlet?"

I have to confess, it made me laugh. It also moved the play along, leaving Jenkins' belligerent Gravedigger to his own thoughts and, apparently, lines. I do not know what is going on between Oxford and Jenkins but the Royal Shakespeare Company (RSC) really needs to get a grip of this seeming clash of personalities. I shall watch developments with interest.

The rest of the review was overwhelmingly positive but the ripples from that evening had reached the artistic director. Jasper Tynan was old school, a director who had paid his dues in regional Rep and worked tirelessly to reach the pinnacle of the RSC. He wasn't about to tolerate anything that would compromise performances.

At nine the next morning, Morris, Richard and I were summoned to a meeting. When I arrived, Morris and Richard were already standing outside his office like naughty schoolboys waiting to see the headmaster.

'Morning.'

They both looked at me and mumbled hello, nobody was in the mood for talking. We stood with an uncomfortable silence hanging between us like a cold fog. Our silence was disturbed by a distant rumble of thunder, which turned out to be Jasper Tynan summoning us into his office. 'Enter.'

The three of us shuffled in, dreading Jasper's wrath, two of us without reason. Jasper sat in his chair, like an emperor upon his throne. He gestured towards three chairs that were lined up in front of his desk. Clearly, we were going to be there for a while.

Jasper waited for us all to be seated and then began. 'Well, gentlemen, what the hell went on last night?'

There was an uncomfortable silence. I looked at Morris and he looked at Richard, who just grinned. This didn't help Jasper's temperament.

'I don't see what there is to smile about, Jenkins. From what I have heard it was you who caused the problem. Explain yourself.'

Richard nodded towards Morris. 'Why don't you ask him!'

'I'm asking you, not Oxford. What's going on?'

Richard turned to gaze out of the window at the river Avon flowing quietly by, clearly unconcerned about the growing storm at its side.

'I think Richard was sulking about his part,' said Morris.

'What part? It was barely a walk on.'

'The Gravedigger scene is a pivotal moment in the play.'

'Which could be played by any competent actor,' snapped Richard.

'Well you certainly didn't manage that last night, did you!'

The gloves were off now and Morris and Richard glared at each other, spoiling for a fight.

Jasper had seen enough. 'Gentlemen, there is obviously something going on between you and we are not leaving this room until it's resolved. Do I make myself clear?'

'Richard was making up his own dialogue. He was having a go at me because he wanted to play Hamlet.'

'No, I didn't. I knew you would never let that part go. I just wanted a proper role, I'm not a spear-carrier any more.'

'Well, you are now,' snapped Morris. 'I will never put you in any role after what you did last night.'

Jasper raised his hand. 'That's enough, gentlemen. It's clear there is a personality clash going on here.' He turned to me. 'You were there, Richards, what are your thoughts?'

Nothing like being put on the spot. They turned to me, both expecting me to take their side. I was in a no–win situation. Jasper had arched his fingers and was flexing them impatiently.

'I think …' I hesitated. What did I think? Richard and Morris were my friends but Morris was also my boss.

'Come on, Richards. I'm dying to know.' Jasper was reaching the end of his limited tether.

'Well, it's quite tricky. Both Richard and Morris are great actors and either could take on the leading role.'

'Quite so, but I note you gave Jenkins top billing then,' said Jasper.

'Er, that wasn't intentional, it could have been the other way around.'

'So, is it Morris or Jenkins then?'

There was a twinkle in Jasper's eye and I realised he was playing with me. I desperately tried to find a way to explain myself without taking sides.

'Both Morris and Richard are great actors but Morris is the principal actor and artistic director of the company so I suppose he must have the final say.' I looked up at Jasper Tynan, hoping he was going to save me from having to tip-toe along the political tightrope I was trying to walk.

Jasper leaned back in his chair. 'If I understand the situation clearly, and I think I do, we have a clear clash between two actors who both want the lead roles. Would that be a fair summation?'

'No, not at all,' protested Richard.

'That was a rhetorical question, Jenkins. I know the answer. You feel that the role of the Gravedigger was unworthy of your talent and yet, I have it on good authority that you have been given the role of Caliban in *The Tempest* this season. Is that correct?'

'Well, I suppose so,' admitted Richard.

'I'll take that as a yes. So, what's your problem, Richard? You want the lead role every time, do you?'

'I never said that, Jasper. I just want a fair shake of the parts. Morris is trying to keep me in the background because he feels threatened.'

'I do not! You are no threat to me.'

Richard turned angrily towards him. 'You've always felt threatened by me, Morris, admit it.'

The whole meeting was descending into chaos.

Jasper held up a hand. 'Gentlemen, this needs to stop. NOW!'

We all sat there; me watching Morris and Richard seething at each other, and Jasper looking between all of us. The silence lasted no more than ten seconds but it felt longer. It was Richard that broke it.

'I'm leaving.'

'Leaving, who said anything about leaving?' demanded Jasper.

I noticed that, after the initial surprise, Morris was fighting to hold back a smile.

'I've been offered Henry V at the Bristol Old Vic.'

'But you are under contract here,' said Jasper. 'You can't leave without my agreement.'

'Henry V, that's a great part.'

Jasper glared at Morris. 'What's that got to do with it?'

'I was just making an observation,' said Morris. 'Old Vic's a bloody good company too,' he added, smiling.

'You see, he can't wait to get rid of me and I can't wait to go.'

'Nobody is going anywhere without my say-so,' snapped Jasper. 'You two can bugger off now. Richards, you stay.'

I had no choice and remained in my seat as they left Jasper's office, both giving me meaningful looks, demanding that I should take their side.

Jasper waited for the door to close before speaking. As it clicked behind the departing thespians, he turned to me and smiled. 'Well now, Felix, we seem to have a clash of egos here, don't we. Which one would you pick?'

It was a terrible question; Richard was my friend but Morris was my boss, and we did get on.

Jasper savoured my discomfort. 'You must have a favourite.'

'They are both amazing in their own way. Morris is a brilliant artistic director and as a leading actor he is superb, really leads the company well.'

'But? I can hear a but, Felix.'

I nodded. 'Richard is the greatest actor I have ever seen. He doesn't even act, he *becomes* the character. He inhabits the role. It's incredible to witness up close. It's seamless.'

'I know, I've seen it. There is a problem with him though, isn't there?'

'Is there?' I shrugged, avoiding a direct answer.

'He's Welsh, isn't he.'

'I don't think that's a problem, Jasper.'

'No, of course not. But he has the Celtic temperament, all moody and hard done by. I bumped into him the other day, and the way he spoke to me, you'd have thought I had just closed his coal mine.'

'I don't think he owns a coal mine, Jasper.'

'Don't be obtuse, Felix, you know exactly what I mean. He's a great artist but he's unstable. That may be where the greatness comes from, but it's dangerous. We can't have a repetition of what happened last night. Next time you might not be there to diffuse it.'

'So, what are you going to do?'

Jasper leaned back in his chair and appeared to consider the situation for a moment, but he was acting. I am certain he had made up his mind before we even entered his office.

He held up a letter. 'This is Jenkins' resignation letter. I'm of a mind to accept it.'

'You can't, Jasper.'

He looked at me reprovingly. 'I think you'll find I can. We have Morris and Sir Miles; two huge stars should be enough for this season, don't you think.'

'I don't agree. Richard is quite simply the best stage actor of his generation, we can't lose him.'

'I'm afraid we can. I'm accepting this letter with immediate effect.'

'What about Beatrice and their baby? He can't leave them here.'

'He's asked to be released from his contract, this is his doing.

If he wants to come back, I am sure we can accommodate him …
at a lower rate.'

I looked into Jasper's eyes. His mind was made up and this
conversation was over. I headed for the door without saying a
word. As I laid my hand upon the door handle, Jasper spoke.

'This means you will get to play Caliban in *The Tempest*. You
see, Felix, there's always a silver lining.' I nodded and left.

My friend, Richard, would be leaving Stratford; he had fallen
for Morris' goading and had taken the bait – hook, line, and
sinker. How would poor Beatrice cope? How would Richard
cope? The whole thing was just a terrible mess.

Chapter 4
A Clash of Kings

Richard's departure had come as a terrible blow to the cast. Despite looking very pleased, Morris gathered us all together that afternoon and did his best to rally the company.

'By now you will all have heard the news that Richard has left us for pastures new. While we regret and mourn his loss, we must celebrate what lies before us. Richard has joined the Bristol Old Vic and I am sure we wish him well.'

'But what about me and Oliver, what will we do?'

Morris smiled sympathetically. 'You are both part of our family, Beatrice. There will always be a place for you here. Richard will have plenty of time between shows to come to Stratford.'

'I'm not sure I can do this on my own,' she whispered.

I was sure she could. Beatrice had a cold hard resilience I had seen before. It could have been determination but I think it was ambition. In a similar situation, most new mothers would have gone with the father of their child, but not Beatrice. Stratford was where her future lay, with or without Richard.

Morris and she would become ever closer as the days after Richard's departure grew to weeks. The company seemed to divide; those that were for Richard staying and those that just went along with Morris. Beatrice seemed to be caught somewhere in the middle, but always deferred to Morris' suggestions. Maybe I should have seen it sooner, but that was where the first signs of toxic love were posted. Morris and Beatrice had entered into an unwritten contract; she had become dependent upon him and he'd welcomed it.

After Richard had finished his run in *Henry V*, I went to meet him in Bristol. His performance had been a triumph, and he had received rave reviews, but I was shocked when I saw him. When he walked into the bar at the King William, he seemed to have shrunk. There was a haunted look to his features. This was not the look of a man who was the toast of the Bristol theatre.

'Bloody hell, Richard, haven't you eaten since you left Stratford?'

He grinned. 'Not much. I had a lot of lines to learn. Now the run's finished, I can get back to normal for a while.'

'Define normal.'

He laughed. 'How can I, I'm an actor. I make a living pretending to be someone I'm not, a bit like when Morris pretends he can act.'

'Oh, that's harsh. He's not as good as you but he's not bad.'

Richard took a long pull on the pint I had lined up for him.

'Have you seen Beatrice and Oliver recently?' I knew he hadn't.

He shrugged. 'It's not easy. Bristol and Stratford aren't exactly close and I don't drive.'

'But you'll go up and see them now the run's over, won't you?'

'If I can.'

'But she needs you, and you need to see your son.'

He shook his head. 'It's not that easy, Felix. I can't go back. Every time I see Morris, it reminds me that he's chased me away from my home; that he's won.'

It was terrible to hear him say it. He belonged on the stage at Stratford, and yet, he was right. Morris had exiled him. Like an ancient king, he had seen the threat and neutralised it. Richard, despite the recent acclaim, was now in a personal wilderness, robbed of his wife and child and the place he craved to be. The inner turmoil was written across his gaunt face.

'I'm not sure Beatrice and I are going to make it.'

'Of course you will, she loves you.'

His laugh was bitter. 'Ha, she loves Stratford more. Morris has her wrapped around his little finger.' Richard turned to me, his face filled with uncertainty. 'Do you think they are having an affair?'

'No, of course not. Why on earth would you think that?'

'Don't you?'

The thought of an affair had never occurred to me but, now Richard had asked, it made me wonder if I'd dismissed things too quickly. I had seen the looks that passed between them; were they more than those that colleagues or friends would exchange? Maybe he was right, but there was no way I could agree with him. He was just too fragile.

'No, I don't. You need to get a grip, Richard. Beatrice and Oliver need you. Go to Stratford and ask Jasper for your job back. After the reviews you've received here, he would love to have you.'

'Morris would never allow it.'

'Morris won't have a choice. Jasper decides who plays at the RSC; if he wants you back, you're in.'

And that is pretty much what happened. Richard was reinstated by Jasper, who made it very clear that any future ad-libbing on stage would not be tolerated. He also guaranteed that Richard would get his share of leading roles. Morris hadn't been happy but, ever the pragmatist, he'd accepted it, playing the long game. Richard would step out of line sooner or later and, until then, he had bigger fish to fry.

When it came to big fish, there were none on the English stage that were bigger than Sir Miles Tennyson. His was the voice of a generation; actually, several generations.

Born in London in 1868, he had performed in front of Queen Victoria many times and starred in Shakespearian roles for over forty years. He was a darling of the nation since his appearance on the cover of the Radio Times, when the BBC broadcast *King Lear* with Sir Miles – who was just Miles back then – in the lead.

The broadcast had a huge audience and there was an interview with him afterwards. He had been suave, debonair, charming but, most of all, he had been funny. I remember listening to the broadcast with Morris and Richard in our digs in Birmingham during the run of *The White Devil* by John Webster. Morris hadn't been happy.

'Can you bloody believe it? Tennyson on the radio! We should ask for our licence money back. That old duffer should be in a museum, not on the BBC.'

Morris was a fine actor but he couldn't disguise his jealousy. Richard and I thought he was being ridiculous, and Richard told him so.

'I don't see why you are getting so worked up, Morris. The old boy's a legend, he deserves his moment in the spotlight.'

'But I'm better!' he protested.

Richard and I looked at each other and then burst into laughter.

'I'm better, I'm better,' mimicked Richard. 'It should have been me.' He slapped the back of his hand to his forehead for dramatic effect. 'I have been usurped!'

'Piss off, the pair of you,' hissed Morris. This had just made us laugh even harder.

Sir Miles was being interviewed by Arnold Weston, the theatre critic for The Times. Richard and I giggled as we watched Morris; he had a severe case of envy.

'Sir Miles Tennyson, you are acknowledged as the greatest living Shakespearian actor. How does that feel?'

'Jesus,' said Morris.

'Humbling, Arnold, very humbling. One hopes that one's toils on the stage are appreciated and it's marvellous to get such acclaim. For me it is not about the fame, it's about the work. The Bard's words are everything.'

Morris threw something at the radio.

'You have to give it to the old boy, he certainly knows how to work a microphone. That felt like he was speaking directly to us. He seems so sincere.'

'He's a bloody actor, he's acting,' cried Morris.

We shushed him as Weston continued. 'Even now, after all these years, it's the work that is most important?'

'Absolutely, Arnold. My whole life has been dedicated to bringing Shakespeare's words to life, inspiring new generations.'

'You don't regret not going into film?'

Sir Miles laughed. 'Good God, no, film holds no allure for me.'

'You mean no bugger wanted you!'

'You do know he can't hear you,' said Richard.

Morris grinned. 'Of course, it's just ... The old boy is so full of crap. He's been trying to get into film for years but he just can't tone it down enough for the camera. He's always projecting to the back of the theatre. Did you see him doing that love scene with Dame Helen Smitten? Nearly blew her out of the bedroom when he declared his love for her!'

We had all seen the film, it was called *Last Chance at Love* and Sir Miles was playing an older gentleman who was trying to woo an ex-wife.

'"Do you love me, Sylvia,"' screamed Morris at the top of his voice. '"Because I love you, I really do."'

We burst out laughing, it was a good impression. Sir Miles had delivered his lines like a sergeant major blasting poor Dame Helen against the wall, like a spider pinned by a hurricane. We couldn't remember the next line but, needless to say, his last chance at film had ended right there.

'Do you think you will ever retire?' asked Weston.

'Never,' said Sir Miles, without a moment's hesitation. 'I shall tread the boards until the day I die.'

'That can be arranged,' said Morris.

Richard and I laughed, never dreaming that he actually meant it.

Chapter 5
The Lesser of Two Evils

For Beatrice Smallman, life had become hard. Her son was only a few months old, and her husband was now working eighty miles away. She had to care for young Oliver on her own while still holding down two roles at the theatre. She was fortunate that her mother lived in town and could support her with childcare, but this also meant she had to listen to her constant criticism of Richard.

I had popped round for a cup of tea one day and witnessed her in action. Beatrice and I were sitting in the kitchen of her flat in Holtom Street when Agatha Smallman swept in.

'Felix, how are things?'

'Fine, thanks, what about you?'

Agatha raised both eyebrows to the ceiling. 'How do you think I am, Felix? I'm having to do Richard's parenting for him. I warned Beatrice about mixed marriages.'

'Mixed marriages?'

'Marrying foreigners,' she explained.

'But Richard's Welsh.'

'Exactly! The Celts; singing, drinking and fighting, totally unreliable.'

It was fair to say that Agatha was a product of the British Empire, her father had owned a tea plantation in the north of India. This probably accounted for her reaction to anyone with anything less than a received English BBC accent. Contempt. I always made sure not to drop a H around her.

'He's had amazing reviews for his role as Willy Loman; have you seen them?'

'I think I saw something about it,' she admitted dismissively.

'He was playing a washed-up character, wasn't he?'

'Yes.'

'Typecasting,' she snapped, and then turned to her daughter. 'I told you nothing good would come from marrying him, didn't I?'

'What about your grandson?'

Agatha looked down at Oliver sleeping quietly in his cot. 'I'll grant you that one, but nothing else.'

'But I love him, Mother,' protested Beatrice.

'I love cake,' snapped Agatha, 'but I'm not going to marry one.'

'That makes no sense, you can't marry a cake.'

Agatha sighed. 'Don't be obtuse, dear, you know exactly what I mean.'

Beatrice looked at me and we both began to laugh.

'I'm sorry, Mother, but I really don't know what you mean. Richard is a great actor.'

'He may be but you can eat a cake, what can you do with a surly Welshman?'

There wasn't really an answer to a question like that so I tried to change the subject. 'Richard will be coming back soon; I think the deal is already signed. Jasper Tynan couldn't wait to get him back from Bristol.'

'I bet that nice Morris Oxford wasn't so happy. If you ask me, Richard is after his job. He would love to be the artistic director.'

'Richard would hate that, Mother, he just wants to act.'

'So does Morris. I told you to marry him but you wouldn't listen.'

'I don't love Morris,' said Beatrice.

Agatha smiled at her the way a vet would at a dog he was about to put down. 'Oh, Beatrice, how can you be so naïve. You don't marry for love, you marry for security. A man with a big belly eats well, which means that *you'll* eat well. A man in a nice suit probably has a house, a house *you* can live in.'

'Richard doesn't have a big belly.'

'Exactly! He's thin, doesn't look like he's had a good meal in years and his clothes ...' Agatha raised her hands in frustration. 'He'd lose a catwalk contest with a scarecrow.'

It was clear she was not a fan of her son-in-law, so I came to his defence.

'Richard is a great artist, Mrs Smallman. He's not bothered by the trappings of success, he just wants to do the work.'

She wasn't convinced by my argument. 'Morris is a great actor and he dresses nicely. He has his own house, too,' she said, pointedly, looking at Beatrice as she did so.

There was nothing Beatrice could say to this, all of it was true. Sitting in that kitchen, she looked thoroughly miserable. She missed Richard so much and motherhood without him was tough. It didn't help that her own mother always referred to him in disparaging terms, and held Morris up as an example of the perfect man.

Little did I know that within two years, Richard would be dead and Beatrice would be living with Morris. Within twenty years they would become Sir and Lady Oxford. That would have all seemed impossible sitting in their kitchen all those years ago, but it happened. All of it.

Chapter 6
The Man Who Would Be King

Morris Oxford was riding high in the spring of 1935. The last two seasons at Stratford had been a triumph, both his acting and his artistic direction had been acclaimed. He was the star of the moment, but there was a blot on his otherwise clear horizon: Sir Miles Tennyson and Richard Jenkins were also receiving great reviews.

Sir Miles was regarded with great affection by everyone and this, Morris believed, led to him being reviewed through rose-tinted glasses. While his performances were still good, they could hardly be described with superlatives. But they were, every bloody night. Morris really was beginning to despise the old buffer, who, despite his age, showed no sign of shuffling off his mortal coil, preserved as he was in fine claret and beef Wellington. Morris needed to play the waiting game but patience wasn't in his nature. There was a remedy to his problem which would come in the unlikely form of Lord Burke of Ponty, but more on that later.

Richard, however, was a different matter. Morris had given him leading parts in *The Tempest* and *As You Like It*. He'd also let him take the lead in an adaptation of *School for Scandal* by Sheridan. Sir Oliver was a part intended for a much older man, but Richard inhabited his character and seemed to age thirty years when he walked on stage.

It was an amazing performance, both funny and moving. Naturally, he received rave reviews but between these roles,

Morris would hide Richard in the lesser roles. It was a clever game.

When Richard complained, he could always point to a lead role he had just played or was about to play.

Meanwhile, Morris was giving himself at least two lead roles per season. His reputation was gradually overwhelming Richard's by sheer weight of exposure. It's only now, with the perspective of time, that I can see this. I was young, we all were, and the life we were living seemed like an impossible dream. It would be another year before this dream became a nightmare. Until that happened, we revelled in our youth, greedily drinking from the fountain of opportunity we had been granted, never imagining it would end. Except Richard; he knew. Morris watched Richard like a hawk, studying his every move, learning from the nuances in his performances. He was like a sponge trying to soak up Richard's brilliance. He absorbed it but he just couldn't use it. Those gifts were God given, you either had them or you didn't. Morris was a fine actor but the gods had not smiled on him as they had Richard, and his frustration grew.

I found him in the Dirty Duck one afternoon. He looked up and smiled a beer-sodden grin, which was unusual for him.

'Felix, fancy a drink, old chap? I've been drowning my sorrows.'

I walked over to the bar and pulled up the stool next to him. 'What on earth have you got to be sad about? You're the toast of the English stage.'

'I am, aren't I.' He didn't sound sure.

'You are, Morris. One day you'll be just like Sir Miles, a national treasure.'

'Do you really think so, Felix? I bloody loathe him. Why won't he die?'

I laughed. 'Can't stand the competition?'

'He's no competition for me. He's a spent force, strutting like a peacock and trading on his reputation. Howling around the stage like a wounded buffalo.'

'He does a good howl, sends shivers down my spine,' I said.

Morris nodded. 'I'll grant you that, his voice is still good but …'

'But what?'

He looked up at me through drink-laden eyes, leaned towards me and whispered, 'He's just too … y'know. Way too.'

I shook my head. 'Way too what?'

'Alive.'

Again, I should have seen it for what it was. Hindsight is a wonderful thing, but useless. We only see it after it's happened. What's the point of that?

'My tragedy, Felix, is that I was born too late and too poor. Sir Miles had too much of a start on me and he came from money. Money buys you influence.' He paused for a moment to drain his glass. 'And now I have Richard to contend with as well.'

I said nothing; what was there to say? We all knew that Richard was the greater actor. Morris was trapped between living history and the greatest talent I had ever witnessed; when you're consumed by ambition, that's not a comfortable place to be.

I had to help Morris back to his digs after we left the pub; his legs were dancing but didn't recognise the tune. He was a big man, even back then but, somehow, I managed it. I laid him on his bed, pulled off his shoes and threw a blanket over him.

'Goodnight, sweet prince, and flights of angels sing thee to thy rest!'

'Bugger off, Felix.'

As I walked down Old Town towards my place on Trinity Street, our conversation played back in my head. Poor Morris was obsessed with Sir Miles' fame and Richard's talent, and yet, he was the toast of Stratford. Like a lot of actors, the one character he was uncomfortable playing was himself. The mirror, when you look into it, never lies. Morris Oxford didn't like what he saw, but there comes a point when you just can't look away. I chuckled at the thought of Morris waiting for Sir Miles to die. Maybe a cold snap would see him off. I doubted it; with the amount of alcohol he kept in his system, he would never freeze.

The summer faded and the trees turned from green to yellow. Autumn leaves fell and, before long, winter season was upon us, along with three new plays: *Othello*, *Richard lll* and *The Merry Wives of Windsor*. Morris hoped to play Sir John Falstaff in *Merry Wives*, but Jasper Tynan had a nasty surprise for him.

Morris had been for his regular planning meeting with Jasper, fully expecting to have the role; he coveted a chance to perform some comedy. To his dismay, Jasper had earmarked Sir Miles for the part.

When Morris found me in the rehearsal room, he was incandescent with rage. 'You won't believe this, Felix. Jasper's given John Falstaff to bloody Sir Miles. It's an outrage.'

'Is it? I think he'd be pretty good.'

'But he's too old to be chasing the wives of Windsor around, he'd never catch them.'

'Isn't that the point? Falstaff is an ageing, corpulent buffoon. His mind is willing but his body can't keep up.'

Morris looked at me, aghast. '*Et tu, Brute*? You think he's a better choice than me?'

'I never said that, Morris. He's a different choice, not a better choice.'

Morris stared at me for a moment in disbelief. 'You really think so?'

I shrugged. 'I don't see why not. Sir Miles is probably only about eight years older than Falstaff would have been in the play and he plays comedy well.'

I thought about saying more but the look on his face stopped me. He slowly shook his head, turned away and walked from the room without another word. If only I had known where he was going, I would have stopped him.

The next time I saw Morris was an hour later in the Dirty Duck. He'd been drinking. He looked pale, flustered. One look at his face sent a chill through my body.

'What's wrong?'

Morris checked the room to make sure we were alone. The barman had disappeared. 'Something terrible has happened.'

I wasn't sure I wanted to know but I heard myself asking him anyway. 'What's happened?'

'It's Sir Miles … He's dead!'

That was a lot to take in. 'Are you sure?'

Morris nodded. 'Yes, out like a light.'

I put my hand on his shoulder. 'Start at the beginning.'

'I knocked on his door and he asked me to come in. Sir Miles was reclined on his couch. I could see a manuscript laying on his chest. It rose and fell with his breathing. I could tell my visit had awoken him from his morning nap.

'"Oh, it's you, Morris," he said as he sat up. "What on earth are you doing here?"

'I was so angry, Felix. I didn't know what to say. He sat up, took the manuscript from his chest and placed it on the table beside him. He saw I was trying to read what it was.

'"*Merry Wives*. Jasper's given me the role of Falstaff."

'He smiled patronisingly at me. You know the way he does. I felt like beating him to death with it.'

Morris was way too young to play Falstaff and he knew it but, like a kid in a sweet shop, when it came to great roles, he wanted them all. There was no reasoning with him when he was like this, so I didn't try.

'Tell me what happened or I'm going.'

Before I even turned to go, Morris grabbed my arm.

'Don't go, I need to tell you something.' There was fear in his eyes and, in an instant, he seemed to have sobered up. He looked around furtively. 'Let's go outside where we won't be overheard.'

He ushered me out to the patio at the front of the Dirty Duck. It was raised up about eight feet above the pavement level so was reasonably quiet. There was nobody out there but us.

Morris moved closer to me. 'Sir Miles is dead.'

I still didn't comprehend the meaning of his words for a moment, but he repeated them.

'Sir Miles really is dead.'

'How?' It was all I could think to say.

'Natural causes, I think.'

'You think? Morris, what the hell are you talking about?'

'Keep your voice down, for God's sake. This is a delicate matter.'

'What's happened?'

Morris shifted from foot to foot. 'I think he had a heart attack.' He paused. 'Or a stroke … and then a fall.' He shook his head. 'Nasty fall.'

'What was he doing, gymnastics?' I leaned in close to Morris. 'You need to tell me exactly what's happened.'

'Nothing's happened, he just—'

'Had a heart attack, a stroke and a terrible fall. Is he definitely dead?'

'I'm not sure, he seemed to be somewhere in between when I left him. There was a bit of gurgling and shaking. Hard to tell, I'm not a doctor.'

'Have you raised the alarm?'

Morris looked sheepish. 'Not yet, I thought I'd have a quick stiffener before I got involved with all that nastiness.'

I couldn't believe my ears. 'You left him alone in that condition and haven't called an ambulance?' He shook his head. 'How long?'

He glanced at his watch. 'No more than an hour.'

'Jesus Christ, Morris, what the hell were you thinking?'

'I didn't really think, I just panicked and ran. You know I hate the sight of blood.'

I grabbed his arm. 'Come on, Morris, we need to get to Sir Miles, fast.'

'Must we?'

'We must!'

Before we could get down the steps, we were greeted by a panting Desmond Tharpe. He charged up them two at a time. 'Have you heard?'

'Heard what?' asked Morris, with an innocence that was breathtaking.

'Sir Miles Tennyson is dead!'

Morris slumped into the nearest chair as if in shock. 'He should have died hereafter. There would have been a time for such a word.'

In that moment, as he quoted from *Macbeth*, I realised he had killed Sir Miles, but what could I do? If I said anything, I would look complicit. Desmond and I looked at Morris; he appeared a broken man. A tear ran down his cheek.

'Tomorrow and Tomorrow and Tomorrow. Creeps in this petty pace from day to day. To the last syllable of recorded time, and all our yesterdays have lighted fools the way to dusty death.'

I watched him in horrified admiration; he was giving the performance of his life.

'He's in shock,' whispered Desmond. 'You stay here with him and I will try to find out more information.'

I nodded in agreement. 'Good idea. I'll stay with Morris, make sure he's all right.'

Desmond squeezed my arm. 'Good man, be back as soon as I can.' He turned, leaped down the steps and disappeared down Southern Lane at a run.

When I turned back to Morris, the tears had turned to a smile. The transformation was stunning.

I sat down opposite him. 'You'd better keep talking, Morris, or I'm going to the police.'

'But—'

'You've got five minutes or it's the police. You choose.'

After a few moments, he scowled. 'Very well, where do you want me to start?'

'Start from where you left off. Sir Miles lying on his sofa with the script on his chest.'

'It was something and nothing. He was rubbing it in my face. Told me I was too young to play Falstaff.'

'You are.'

'I didn't see it that way. I grabbed the manuscript and threw it on the fire.'

'He has an open fire in his dressing room?'

Morris shook his head. 'No, it's a two-bar electric fire, I was being symbolic.'

'You were being a prat. What happened next?'

'The old git got up, laughed in my face and then launched into a speech.'

'What did he say?'

'That I was just a jumped-up idiot who had done nothing to earn my reputation and was more interested in playing me than playing Shakespeare's characters as he had written them. Apparently, he thought I had made Shakespeare's characters subservient to my interpretation. Can you believe it?'

I could but, at this particular moment, I didn't think my opinion would be helpful. 'Go on.'

'Well, the moment I threw his script onto the metaphorical flames, I calmed down. I realised I was being stupid. I was going to apologise, but he turned on me. I bent down to pick up the script and he slapped me across the back of the head.

'"Who the hell do you think you are? I've trod these boards for decades. I've forgotten more lines than you'll ever know. You think you are really something, don't you, but I have worked with the greats. Gielgud, Barrymore, Beerbohm, Beatrice Patrick-Campbell. These are true greats, not Johnny-come-lately like you.

You are not worthy to carry their swords."

'I stood up with the pages I had gathered and offered them to him … and he laughed in my face.

"'I don't need those. I already know the text, I just wanted the stage directions. You can take those and shove them where the sun don't shine."

'He threw them at me imperiously, shouting triumphantly as he did so. "Now, bugger off!" He went to turn away from me and then suddenly stopped. He clutched his chest, swayed for a moment and then began to fall. Our eyes met as he fell and I could see he knew this was serious. "Help me," he mouthed. His head struck the edge of the fire with a sickening crack, stunning him and splitting his skull.

'I went to the door to call for help but, when I looked down the corridor, there was nobody there. Our argument had gone unheard. I waited for another couple of minutes and no one came. I couldn't believe it. I went back in and closed the door behind me. His breathing had become laboured and his lips were starting to turn blue. As I leaned over him, his eyes opened and he looked directly at me. "You will never wear the crown."

'His whispered words were full of venom. For a moment, I thought about trying to help him but there was blood everywhere. If I got any on me, the police may think I had something to do with it. I stood up and watched the light slowly drain from him. He tried to raise his hand but it was shaking too much. He repeated, "Help me." Those were his last words. After that, his breathing became erratic. I wiped down every surface I had touched and then headed for the pub.'

I sat there in silent disbelief. Did I even know this man?

'Say something, Felix.'

'I can't believe you just left him there to die. What's wrong with you!'

'Oh, come on. Put yourself in my shoes.'

'I'd rather not.'

'Don't judge me, Felix. Imagine how it would look if anybody had heard us arguing. I had no choice.'

'There wasn't a choice to be made,' I snapped. 'Sir Miles needed your help and you turned your back on him. It's murder by neglect.'

'That would make a good title for a play.'

I slapped him, hard, across the face, the impact echoed down Southern Lane.

Morris recoiled, holding his cheek. 'What the hell did you do that for?'

'To knock some sense into you. A man is dead and you watched him die. Have you no shame?'

'That hurt.'

'It was meant to.'

Morris rubbed his cheek and winced. There are a lot of nerve endings in the face and, judging by the blood rushing to the surface, I'd woken up all of his.

'Look, I'm sorry, but he was old, it was natural causes. Sure, we had a bit of a row but that's not illegal. Artistic differences, that's all.'

'Maybe it was, right up to the point that you looked down the corridor, saw nobody was coming and then shut the door.' I raised my hand and pointed at him. 'You wanted him to die.'

I watched his face as he considered my accusation; it was conflicted. He wanted to deny it but he just couldn't.

He sighed. 'Very well. I did want him to die. That doesn't make me a bad person, does it?'

'Yes, it bloody well does. It's cold, callous, calculating. I'm not sure I know who you are any more.'

'Do you doubt me, Felix?'

'Of course I do! You just left a man to die. You're evil.'

He laughed. 'That's such an ugly word. What happened to Sir Miles was an accident; natural causes. Maybe I could have got help but it wouldn't have made any difference. He was turning blue, you should have seen him. In fact, you did see him, didn't you.'

This was a nightmare; Morris was actually threatening to drag me into this if I spoke to the police!

He pulled his chair up close and smiled; it was one of his better ones. 'Look, do you believe that it happened just as I said?' I nodded. 'Good. So, you know I didn't kill him, I just left the scene without raising the alarm. Why don't we just leave it there and see what happens? If somebody saw me then I'll have to tell them what I just told you, if not ...' he shrugged. 'Case closed.'

There wasn't really a lot I could say to that. Morris was my friend and boss. 'You think that's the right thing to do?'

'Sins of omission. Not much of a sin, is it?' He looked at me thoughtfully, as if assessing what to say next. 'There is a positive to take from this ... tragedy.'

'And what's that, Morris?'

'Dead men's shoes. Everyone gets to take a step up, you too.'

There was no mistaking his offer: for my silence, I would be rewarded with bigger parts, a chance to star. In life, we sometimes come to a fork in the road, we can choose the right way or the wrong way. That day, I put myself on the wrong side of history for a handful of silver and a moment in the spotlight.

In the years since, I have tried to justify my silence but the mirror never lies – I have never really recovered. The reflection I always see is of greed, ambition and the sins of omission. The price was too high.

Chapter 7
Dead Men's Shoes

Morris had been true to his word and bigger roles had opened up before me; I was well rewarded for my silence. Only two people knew that Morris had been with Sir Miles when he had collapsed. There was an unquiet corner of my mind that wondered if he had fallen or if Morris had pushed him. I tried to dismiss it but, late at night, when sleep wouldn't come, it prayed on my mind like a cancer. Always there in the background, eating away at my very soul.

Morris hadn't wasted time. He had studied Sir Miles for years and knew he had everything the old boy had and then some. The talent, the charisma, the voice … He lacked just one thing: the money. Sir Miles came from money and with money came influence. He could afford to surround himself with the best people, even Morris had received a personal stipend from Sir Miles when he was younger. He often supplemented the wages of the company around him; it bought him loyalty and talent that was there to support, not challenge.

He was also known to wine and dine those that would sit in judgement of him; the critics. It was subtle, insidious, he formed attachments that insulated him from criticism and heightened the praise when it was due. It was very hard to give a bad notice to someone you had shared a fine claret with over a meal at The Ritz. Morris had seen all of this and had learned well, but he would take it to the next level in his pursuit of greatness. Not for him, the influential dinners with the gentlemen of the press; he wanted members of the press who were actually on his payroll. Nothing less than his own press corps. It seemed impossible but I watched him do it, and this is where Lord Burke of Ponty joins our tale.

To achieve what Morris wanted he needed money but, as he was not from money, he needed patronage. A person of standing with a cheque book big enough to finance a small country. I remember sitting in the Dirty Duck a few days after Sir Miles' death, as he passed me a copy of The Times.

'Look who's coming to town.'

On the inside page was a photo of Lord Leo Burke sweeping into Claridge's like a great general entering the capital of a country he had just conquered. The headline read, *Lord Burke of Ponty returns to London*.

I knew who he was, we all did. There had been rumours that he, like our abdicated king, had become an appeaser of Hitler. Lord Burke had returned from South Africa to prove those rumours wrong.

'Do you believe him?'

'Believe him about what?'

'That he's back to help in the fight against Hitler.'

'Sounds like you don't,' said Morris.

I laughed. 'He has gold mines in Africa, tea plantations in India, and investments all over Europe. The sceptical amongst us think he's just trying to protect his assets and sees good old Blighty as his best bet.'

'They may be right,' said Morris, 'but at least he has come home and he's putting his money where it's needed.'

'I heard most of it was in bank accounts in Switzerland.'

'Don't you like him, Felix?'

'I don't know him but everything I have heard about him leads me to think he's a bit dodgy. The wealth he inherited came from his father. The gold mine owners in Africa were said to treat their workers almost as slaves, living in shanty towns scattered at the edge of the excavations. His tea plantation is just the same. He's the worst kind of imperialist exploiter.'

Morris held up a hand. 'Hold on just a second, don't conflate Lord Burke with his father. He's a totally different proposition altogether.'

'How would you know, Morris?'

'Because I met him in London last week.'

I was stunned. Lord Burke was infamous, a darling of the press and a playboy of the western world. The courter of beautiful women and the husband of none. He was also rumoured to be a man with dubious investments. There were question marks about his character but, in these dark times, with storm clouds gathering over Europe, the return of a prodigal son was to be welcomed. The questions would remain unasked if his fortune was used to help the country in its darkest hour, but what on earth would he want with Morris? I asked the question. 'Why?'

'He wants to be a patron of the arts.'

'And.'

'He is going to be our benefactor, underwrite shows we want to put on in the West End. In short, Felix, our little company has the backing of one of the richest men in Europe.'

I didn't know how he had pulled it off but he had. Morris now had the money behind him to implement his plan. How pure that money was, I would soon discover. For now, though, I would remain silent, watching, as Morris Oxford began to build the foundations of an empire. He was our Caesar, and Stratford his Rome.

Richard was back with the company and he, too, had stepped up. Morris was clearly the star but Richard was getting great reviews.

For my part, I was happy. My roles had improved and so had my income but, more importantly, I was finally gaining recognition, especially for comedy, and no roles or amounts could compete with that. All this went a little way to soothe my conscience, though the guilt never left me; always lurking in the background, like someone else's shadow. I threw myself into the work and, for a while, things went well. The company was happy and the world seemed a wonderful place, full of opportunities.

Our blissful existence in Stratford would not last. It was the spring of 1936 and the world stood on the brink. In Spain, a vicious civil war had begun that would claim the lives of over half a million people, the horror inspiring Picasso to create *Guernica*.

Being an actor seemed frivolous and I had made up my mind to volunteer when the time came. Until then, our little corner of the world remained relatively untroubled, or so I thought. The coroner had decided that Sir Miles' manner of death was natural causes. I breathed a sigh of relief, although I still felt complicit. But, in what – a murder or a calculated act of neglect? The two felt terribly similar.

After two weeks, the day of Sir Miles' funeral had arrived. He was to be buried in Holy Trinity, the church in Stratford where Shakespeare was interred. It had been one of his long-held wishes. His final wish, for help, had been ignored.

It was a beautiful, crisp spring morning. The sun was breaking through the soft mist that rose off the Avon, spilling shafts of light across the graveyard. I stopped and stared for a moment, trying to capture it in my memory and hold it forever. Bathed in the filtered sunlight, the graveyard looked like the scene from a Turner. Sir Miles' hearse was drawn by two beautiful grey mares that appeared through the mist from the top end of Old Town. It was a scene that could have been plucked from the previous century. Sir Miles was well loved, and the great and the good of British theatre were all there, but it was Morris who had caught my eye. He seemed to have taken charge.

Sir Miles had been a confirmed bachelor, which was 1930's code for homosexual. In the absence of family, Morris had taken it upon himself to organise the whole damn thing. Given the possibility that he had murdered Sir Miles, it seemed a little ironic. I had to admire him though, he appeared genuinely moved. That's the beauty of sincerity; once you can fake it, the world's your oyster.

I fell in step beside Richard as we slowly made our way down the treelined path to the church.

'Morris is in his element,' he observed.

'Yes, seems to be enjoying himself.'

Richard grinned. 'Not every day you get a chance to upstage a corpse. Mind you, I reckon that, even dead, Sir Miles could outact him.'

I stifled a laugh, which I managed to turn into a choke; it made my eyes water. An old dear behind me tapped me on the back and, when I turned around, offered me a tissue.

'Never mind, dear, he's in a better place now.'

I nodded my thanks, accepted the tissue and quickly buried my face in it to hide my grin.

Beside me, Richard was struggling to suppress his laughter. When he did, he leaned across and whispered to me, 'You think he really did die of natural causes?'

'What makes you say that?'

He shrugged. 'Seems a bit too convenient to me. Sir Miles seemed fighting fit when I saw him the day before.'

'You a doctor now, then?'

'No, I've got a good bedside manner, though.'

We both laughed and the ladies behind us tutted.

The service had been one of joyful celebration for a life that was well lived and full, and then it came time for Morris to give the eulogy. I watched him make his way to the front and knew we were in for a performance; with the world's press packed into Holy Trinity, I should have expected it. Richard had realised it too.

'Fasten your seat belt, we're in for a bumpy ride.'

When he reached the pulpit, Morris gazed slowly around the church, making direct eye contact with those looking up at him. There were tears in his eyes; the man could act.

'Sir Miles Tennyson was my friend, my mentor, my rock.'

Jesus Christ, the man was raising hypocrisy to levels never before thought of.

'I have looked up to him since I was a child of ten and knew I wanted to act. He was the benchmark, the pinnacle we all sought to reach. He stood atop the mountain and was not aloof, he wanted us all to be there with him.'

This was a lie. Sir Miles was as protective of his position as Morris; he had worked hard to get to the top and he wasn't about to share that with anyone, unless he had to. Richard and I glanced at each other. We didn't recognise the person he was describing as Sir Miles, and he was just getting started.

'The world of the stage will never be the same, it will never see his like again. His was a once and forever talent. Personally, I don't know how I will go on.' His voice broke and he cleared his throat. 'But I will; it's what he would have wanted.'

No, it's not, I thought. He'd have liked you to be in that box, with him reading your eulogy. But truth and facts were never going to feature in Morris' tribute. He was on a roll now; he had a captive audience and the sound of his own voice echoing back at him from the ancient walls of the church. This must have been paradise for him. I settled in for the long haul.

There were anecdotes, some of which were true. Quotes from Shakespeare's plays and sonnets and now, after nearly twenty minutes, he appeared to be nearing the end. I gave Richard a nudge; he had drifted off some minutes before.

'He's wrapping it up,' I hissed.

'Good job. If he left it much longer, we could have been dead too!'

Morris dabbed at his dry eyes. 'I learned the other day that Sir Miles was actually born in the Rhondda Valley.'

'Bugger me,' said Richard.

I kicked him discreetly on the ankle. 'Shut up, I want to hear this.'

Up in the pulpit, Morris continued. 'His parents were not Welsh. His father was an accountant, there to organise the closing of a particular pit for his boss, Lord Aberdare, who owned many of the mines back then. His heavily pregnant wife had joined him on the trip from London, jumping at the chance to spend a few restful days on the Gower. Baby Miles had other ideas though and appeared in the early hours of April the eleventh.' There was a smattering of laughter in the congregation. 'Making Miles half Welsh. Who knew?'

From the looks on the faces around me, nobody.

'Given this, I would like to quote the words of Bread of Heaven, Cwm Rhondda.' Morris shuffled his notes and began to recite.

"'Guide me, O thou great Jehovah,

Pilgrim through this barren land;

I am weak, but thou art mighty,

Hold me with thy powerful hand;'"

And that was as far as he got. Beside me, Richard stood up and, in a beautiful tenor voice, took up the chorus.

"'Bread of heaven, bread of heaven,

Feed me till I want no more;

Feed me till I want no more.'"

Every head had turned towards him as his voice resonated around the church; it was a beautiful and poignant moment.

"'Open now the crystal fountain

Whence the healing stream doth flow;

Let the fire and cloudy pillar

Lead me all my journey through:

Strong deliverer, strong deliverer;

Be thou still my strength and shield;

Be thou still my strength and shield.'"

Richard sang the hymn to its finish, unaccompanied. It was one of the most beautiful things I had ever heard. Sung with real passion and feeling, there wasn't a dry eye in the church. When he had finished, he simply sat down.

For a moment, the congregation sat in silence and then the applause started. Joyous and sincere, it went on for a long time. Richard had to stand up to acknowledge the applause. As it intensified, all eyes were upon him, except mine. I was watching Morris and he wasn't happy. In fact, he looked like he wanted to kill Richard. His thunder had been stolen and his eulogy had been totally forgotten by all, lost to the spontaneous beauty of Richard's singing. That, I realised, was the final nail in Richard's coffin. He would be dead before the year ended, but his career had finished right there.

Chapter 8
The Key to Sorrow

The great and the good headed for the reception. I went to follow but Richard held me back.

'Let's go to the Dirty Duck.'

'But there's a full buffet laid on at the Falcon.'

'Do you think Sir Miles would rather we raise a glass to him in the actors' bar or go along with a bunch of local worthies and press, half of whom have never met him and virtually none of whom have ever stood on a stage with him?'

I nodded. 'You're right, let's go.'

It was quiet in the bar but Stan Mayrick had opened early as a mark of respect for a man who had spent many hours in his pub sacrificing his liver. He pushed two pints across the counter towards us.

'Those two are on the house, gents. You both acted with Sir Miles, didn't you.' We nodded. 'Then you can tell me a few stories about the old boy that the papers don't know.'

Richard smiled at me. 'Well, I have a story, but you can never tell.'

'My lips are sealed,' said Stan.

I got comfortable and settled down for Richard's tale; by the look on his face, it was going to be a good one.

'Do you get to the theatre much, Stan?'

'Not as much as I'd like, the pub keeps me pretty busy most evenings.'

'But you do go?'

'I see two or three plays a year.'

'Did you see him as Falstaff in *Merry Wives* four years ago?'

'I did, he was hilarious.'

'He was, but he nearly missed half of his performance. Sir Miles, as you know, was fond of a small libation. Well, on this night, he'd definitely overdone the lunchtime medication. Do you remember the scene in the play where he has to dive into the trunk to avoid being caught by one of the wives' husbands?' Stan nodded. 'The trunk gets wheeled off stage and then Sir Miles is supposed to climb out and change into a tattered dirty suit but, instead, he falls asleep in the trunk. He'd told the stage hand to, "Bugger off and let me have ten minutes' kip."

The kid was new and forgot to go back and wake him. When we got to the scene where he reappeared, supposedly dishevelled, he hurried back on stage looking pristine. We all stood there looking at him – if he's not dishevelled, the next few lines of dialogue will make no sense – then he brushes the front of his jacket, looks out at the audience, and says, "Those new express dry-cleaners on the corner of Bull Street are damn efficient. I looked like a shower of shit twenty minutes ago, now look at me."

The audience laughed and then he dropped into the dialogue as if nothing had happened. Even the critic from *The Herald* thought it was a deliberate ad-lib.'

Stan nodded. 'Your turn, Felix.'

I thought for a moment. I hadn't acted much with Sir Miles but there was one story.

'I remember, one night, he was on stage playing Sir Toby Belch. I was playing opposite him and he was the most convincing drunk I'd ever seen. Acting drunk isn't easy, most actors overdo it, but he had it nailed. Afterwards, I remember asking him how he managed to act being drunk so convincingly.

'The secret, dear boy, is not to act.'

'Underplay it, you mean?'

He shook his head. 'No, no, dear boy. Don't act at all. *Be* drunk.'

'You were drunk?' I was astounded. His performance had been flawless, he'd never missed a beat.

He held up a cautionary finger. 'But never *too* drunk; it's a fine line.'

Then he winked at me and left the changing room, headed for here before last orders.'

Stan chuckled. 'We'll not see his like again.'

'Oh, I don't know about that,' said Richard. He raised his glass. 'To Sir Miles.'

'Sir Miles,' we echoed. A couple more punters came into the bar and Stan was pulled away from our celebration. Richard and I made our way to a corner table and settled down for the rest of the afternoon; there was no show tonight as a mark of respect.

'Sir Miles would much rather we celebrate him here than in the theatre, this was his spiritual home. It was probably only the claret that kept him alive for the last few years.'

'He was pretty good, wasn't he.'

Richard considered it for a moment. 'He was of his time. Morris is like him, they both play an outline of the character that Shakespeare wrote. It's the way it was done then.'

'So, what's changed?'

'We are trying to get to the real character, the underlying motives for their actions.'

'Making it real.'

'Yeah, I suppose so. Have you studied Stanislavski?' I nodded. 'Well, that's what it's all about for me. Emotional truth, getting into the real depths of any character. Becoming the character you are playing, not just an image.'

'How do you tap into the emotion? I watched you playing Hamlet at Bristol and I couldn't get over the raw emotion you brought to the part. Where did that come from?'

He looked at me with genuine sadness. 'Life.'

'Bloody hell! You seemed totally emotionally destroyed.'

'Not directly but something happened to my family and it's left scars.'

'Can you talk about it?'

Richard smiled. 'Yeah, it was 1856. I think I'm over it.'

'What happened?' I really wanted to know what Richard had tapped into to find such raw emotion.

'Cymmer Colliery disaster. One hundred and fourteen miners died, including my great, great grandfather, his brother and two of his sons. The Rhondda Valley was a vale of tears for many years after that.'

It was stunning, how could one family process such loss? 'So it was an accident?'

Richard shook his head sadly. 'Same old story, the owner didn't provide up-to-date safety gear. Davy lamps were available but he sent his miners into the pit with burning torches. The ventilation of the pit was inadequate and there was a build-up of gas. Just after the morning shift had gone into the pit, there was a huge explosion. The entrance to the mine was blocked and all one hundred and fourteen miners were trapped. Most of them survived the initial explosion but it took three hours for the rescuers to break through the debris.'

'How come they were all dead? Three hours isn't a long time.'

'It is when there's no ventilation and the entrance is sealed. The fire after the explosion burned most of the remaining oxygen. When the rescuers reached them, the miners were grouped together in bunches. Whenever I need to cry or show sadness, I try to imagine that scene: my great, great grandfather finding his brother and his two sons after the explosion. Lying together, holding hands, seeking comfort in their loved ones as they died. There must have been hope but, as one hour became two and nobody came, the realisation that this would be their tomb would have become a reality.

'Imagine watching your sons dying and knowing you couldn't save them. All you could do was comfort them. Helpless, trapped, the outside world a distant dream. A horrible realisation that none of you would ever see the sun again. It's almost unimaginable but, when I try to tap into the true helpless horror of being trapped in that mine, I guess I find a place where desolation lives. It descends upon me like a dark cloud, blocking out all hope.'

I was stunned, it really was unimaginable. The price that had been paid for coal over the years was terrible.

'How do you move on after something like that?'

Richard laughed bitterly. 'You don't, there was no compensation in those days. The mine owner and his staff were found not guilty of negligence by a judge who was an acquaintance. He was a wealthy land owner and there were two laws back then; one for the rich and one for the poor.'

I knew then where some of Richard's greatness came from; I had nothing like that I could draw from, and I was grateful for it.

'What do you tap into when you need to play sad, Felix?'

'I had a goldfish that died.'

Richard burst out laughing. 'And that's why you should play comedy.'

Chapter 9
The Silent Witness

Two weeks later, Morris still hadn't recovered from his disappointment. The BBC had been at the funeral and a film of Richard singing Cwm Rhondda had dominated the news coverage. Morris' eulogy had been mentioned, but only because it had led to Richard's spontaneous outburst. His ego had crashed and burned like the Hindenburg would the very next year.

His dislike of Richard had intensified to the point where he didn't even try to justify it any more. He left him out of *Coriolanus* and *Richard lll* without any justification, and Richard began to sink into a deep depression. He tried to get back to the Old Vic in Bristol but they were still upset that he had returned to Stratford. All the doors were slowly slamming in his face.

Beatrice watched this happen and could do nothing to help. With her responsibilities as Oliver's mother, and roles in two plays, there wasn't much time left to support Richard as the 'black dog' descended upon him. She did, however, have one card left to play and I heard her play it.

It was late at night, as I watched the river Avon flow by. From where I sat on a bench by the Chain Ferry, I heard Morris' voice drifting across the road as he left the Dirty Duck. Suddenly, I heard a shout from about twenty yards away.

'Morris. Morris!'

I recognised the voice at once; it was Beatrice.

Morris peered into the darkness. 'Is that you, Beatrice?'

'Yes, over here.'

I felt like I was about to intrude on something private, so I hurried into the trees that lined Southern Lane. Morris crossed to Beatrice, but she had walked into the park and was waiting in the very place I had been sitting. As I stood in the shadows, just a few yards behind the bench, I wondered how I would explain my presence if they spotted me.

Morris approached her. 'What on earth are you doing here, Beatrice?'

'I need to talk to you.'

'You should have come into the pub.'

'No, I need to talk to you alone, in a place where no one can hear us.'

My desire not to be seen became even more important.

'What on earth could be so serious that we need to talk here?'

'I heard you argue with Sir Miles.'

She said it in such a matter-of-fact way that the implication of her words did not register.

Morris, however, understood immediately. 'I'm sorry?'

'You heard, Morris. I was in the office next door trying to learn my lines. I heard the whole thing.'

'Oh, I see. Why didn't you say something?'

'Because I don't want you arrested for murder.'

Morris laughed; it was hollow. 'Murder! That's a bit strong, isn't it?'

'Do you think so? I heard him fall, Morris. I heard the door open and close, and I doubt you were checking to see if anyone was coming. Not the actions of an innocent man.'

Morris became flustered. 'Now look here, Beatrice, you, you can't just go around making accusations like that. It's—'

'The truth.'

Her words hit Morris like a blow and he visibly swayed. I thought for a moment that he was going to fall, but he steadied himself.

'Look, Beatie, darling,' he stepped towards her.

She held up her hand. 'That's close enough, Morris.'

'Oh, come on, you can't seriously think that I could ever hurt you?'

'I didn't but, having heard you with Sir Miles, I'm not so sure. You're not the person I thought you were, Morris. There is something of the night about you, a ruthless streak.'

Morris laughed, but it was forced, acted. For a few moments, he stood looking at Beatrice, who was slowly backing away from him.

'What do you want, Beatrice?' She stopped. 'Well, what do you want? You haven't confronted me by the river in the dead of night to ask for my beef Wellington recipe.'

Morris' beef Wellington was legendary.

'Tell me exactly what happened and then I'll tell you.' Beatrice seemed to have rallied, her timidity had gone.

Morris sighed. 'Sir Miles and I were discussing him playing Falstaff. I thought it would be too taxing for him.'

'You mean *you* wanted to play Falstaff.'

Morris winced. 'Yes, that too, but it *is* a very taxing role for an older gentleman.'

'The truth, Morris,' insisted Beatrice.

'Very well. We argued. I thought it was time for him to retire, become the elder statesman. Let the next generation take its turn.'

'Like you will?'

'Of course.'

'What happened?'

'We argued but you heard that, didn't you. There was no malice, just a disagreement between colleagues. It became quite heated and I had decided to leave when Sir Miles suddenly seemed to have some sort of episode. He hit the floor before I could reach him. I ran to the door to call for help and …'

'And what?'

'There was no one there.'

'Why didn't you call out?'

'I'm not sure. I closed the door and went back to him. He was struggling to speak; I thought for a moment he'd had a stroke. That would have been terrible for a great actor, known for his great voice. I can't explain or justify this but the idea came into my head that it would be a kindness to just let nature take its course. Let Sir Miles slip away quietly without having to suffer the humiliation of no longer being able to do the thing he loved.' Morris wiped a hand across his brow which, despite the cool of the evening, was covered in beads of sweat. 'I'm ashamed to admit … I left him there and went to the pub, I didn't know what to do.'

Beatrice began a slow hand clap. 'Bravo, Morris, one of your finest performances, you almost had me convinced for a moment.'

Morris beamed. 'Did I?'

'No.' Her voice was cold. 'You and I are alike, Morris. I don't like it but I see it. We both have something that the other wants.'

'And what do you actually want from me for your silence, Beatrice? That's what it's for, isn't it?'

Beatrice shrugged. 'I suppose you could put it like that.'

'Blackmail, that's how I'd put it,' snapped Morris.

'Well, if you were innocent there wouldn't be anything to blackmail you with. I'll take that as an admission of guilt.'

'Cut to the chase, Beatrice. What do you want?'

'I want to play comedy.'

'That's not how I see you.'

'I know. You think I'm just a spear-carrier, but I could be so much more than that, you know I could.'

Morris thought about it for a few moments. 'If I do this, our secret is safe?'

'You have my word on it.'

Morris laughed. 'The word of a liar, now there is a comfort.'

'Up to you. Take it or leave it.'

'And if I do take it, give you the roles you want, what do I get?'

'Me!'

Morris gasped, and so did I.

'I beg your pardon?'

'Me, Morris, you can have me. I know you want me back.'

Morris was struck dumb by her revelation, as was I. Richard's wife was offering herself to Morris in exchange for leading roles in Shakespeare's comedies.

'What about Richard?'

'He's nothing to do with this, this is between you and I.'

Morris seemed confused. 'Let me get this straight, if I start giving you bigger roles—'

'In comedies,' she cut in.

'Then you will,' he gestured towards her, 'come back to me?'

'I'll have sex with you, Morris. Is that clear enough for you?'

Morris sighed. 'You and I, lovers?'

'I never said that. We can have sex, it's not love. I love Richard.'

'You've got a funny way of showing it.'

Beatrice moved closer to Morris. 'This is a transaction, Morris. I get what I want so you get what you want and nobody ever finds out what happened between you and Sir Miles.'

'You are full of surprises, Beatrice.'

'And you left a man to die.'

They stood and looked at each other, the deal done, an unholy contract entered into.

Morris opened his arms. 'Shall we begin,' he grinned.

Beatrice stepped back. 'When I see my name on a good role. Like I said, Morris, this isn't love, it's a transaction.' She turned on her heel, walked out of the park and back down Southern Lane towards the theatre.

'You can come out now, Felix,' said Morris. I didn't move. Morris peered into the dark. 'I saw you go into the park from the pub.'

I stepped forward. 'I didn't know what to do when Beatrice called you, so I panicked and hid.'

Morris laughed. 'No need for apologies, old chap, you are the only person who already knew the truth. Who'd have thought that little Beatie could be so calculating? Still, at least it gets me off the hook and, as an added bonus, I get to enjoy the lovely Beatrice. A win—win if ever there was one.'

'You can't be serious? She's Richard's wife!'

Morris held up his hands in defence. 'You heard her, Felix. If I don't have sex with her, she'll go to the police. I have no choice.'

'You could just give her the role.'

Morris grimaced. 'I suppose I could, but where's the fun in that? I've been wanting to get my leg over Beatrice again for ages.'

I was appalled. 'Have you no morals?'

'No, apparently not. Still, all's well that ends well.' Morris winked at me, turned on his heel and disappeared into the night, whistling tunelessly. I stayed there until I couldn't hear him any more.

Chapter 10
A Deal with the Devil

Within a week, Morris had announced the cast for *A Midsummer Night's Dream*. Beatrice had been cast as Titania; the first part of the contract had been fulfilled.

From that day, and all through the rehearsals, I watched the two of them like a hawk, trying to pick up signs that the full contract had been sealed. Nothing seemed to have changed but everything had.

Richard wasn't in *Dream* and had slunk off into the bottom of a bottle. Morris seemed in exceptionally high spirits and Beatrice had been … surprisingly good. Comedy suited her.

I was surrounded by a happy company, but I found no joy in the work. I was playing Quince, a great part, full of humour, but the secrets I carried weighed me down. My best friend was drifting into an alcoholic depression, his wife was having an affair with my boss, and Morris had, at the very best, left Sir Miles to die. It was too much to carry. My fellow actors began to notice and then one day, after rehearsal, Morris asked me to come to his office.

He slumped down behind his desk and pulled a bottle of whiskey and two glasses from a drawer. 'Drink?'

I shook my head. 'No.'

Morris poured one for me anyway. 'You need it, Felix. People are starting to notice your mood. Could you try to brighten up a bit? Your long face is awfully depressing.'

I took the glass from him and drained it. 'You're sleeping with my best friend's wife.'

He grinned. 'We don't do much sleeping. Beatrice is a wild one!'

'My God.' I couldn't hide my disgust. 'You didn't take long, did you?'

'Strike while the iron's hot, old boy, before she changes her mind.'

'So, what now? If Richard finds out, he'll kill you.'

'Richard? I doubt it, he can't see beyond the bottom of a bottle and Beatrice is enjoying herself. I really think I've been good for her.'

'Listen to yourself! It's Richard's wife you're talking about. Imagine if the press got hold of this, they'd crucify you.'

He actually winked at me. 'If you don't tell, I won't.'

He had me; if I ever spoke a word, I would be implicated in the death of Sir Miles. I knew the truth and had said nothing; he had made me complicit in his lie. Morris was weaving a huge web and, one by one, we were being drawn into it. First, me and then Beatrice. Desmond had jumped in voluntarily; he wanted the work and the proximity to fame that Morris provided. If you were in his company, your status was assured. Actors longed for the call from Morris, he was the Pied Piper and we all danced to his tune. This was the beginning of his empire. I tried one more time to reason with him.

'You have to stop this affair, it's not fair to Richard.'

'Look, Felix, you're a decent chap but you lack vision. I'm building something here; audiences and critics will talk about this for years to come. A golden age of the English stage, don't you want to be a part of it?'

Was that a question or a threat? 'You know I do.'

'Well, smile then. Look like you are enjoying yourself – this is Camelot!'

'There's no round table here, Morris. You sit at the head and we are all below the salt.'

Morris chuckled. 'Somebody's got to be the boss, Felix, and I am rather good at it. Why not just get on board and enjoy the ride? Who knows where it's going to lead?'

'Prison.'

'Why so negative? Sir Miles is dead and Richard is finished. Think of the opportunities that are opening up. Your star is rising, Felix, as is mine. With Sir Miles and Richard out of the way, who knows what the limits are!'

And there it was, open and unashamed. Morris saw Sir Miles' death and Richard's mental breakdown as an opportunity. There was no remorse, no empathy. It was all about him. I sat in silence for a long period, not knowing what to say. Morris waited; he had shown his hand and he wanted to know how I was going to react. I wasn't sure myself.

'Come to dinner tonight. There are some people I would like you to meet.'

'No. I'm not in the mood and, to be honest, I'm not sure I want to be around you at the moment, Morris.' I picked up my whiskey and took a swig.

'I can understand that. Richard is your friend, you think I have treated him badly.'

'You have,' I snapped back at him, more aggressively than I had intended. 'You're also sleeping with his wife. You're a disgrace.'

'I may well be, but I have it all now, Felix. You can either get on board or the train will leave the station without you. I want you with me. I value your talent and friendship. The sky's the limit.'

'I thought we were going by train.'

Morris laughed. 'That's why we need you. Nobody plays comedy like you, Felix. Come to dinner, meet my other guests and then make your decision.'

'What's on the menu?'

'Fillet steak.'

'You can't afford fillet steak.'

'I won't be paying, Lord Burke of Ponty will.'

I nearly spat my drink out. 'Lord Burke will be there?'

'Yes, he wants to meet you.'

'Why would he want to meet me?'

'Because you're Felix Richards. Lord Burke is a fan of Shakespeare, especially the comedies, and that makes him a fan of yours too.'

I was struggling to take on board what Morris was telling me. You have to remember that, back then, Lord Burke was one of the most famous people in Europe and his wealth was legendary. 'What time?'

Morris grinned, he had me hooked. 'Seven o'clock. Bring your appetite, your ambition and an open mind.'

Four hours later, I walked into the lounge at The White Swan and there, seated at a table with Morris, was a man I had only seen on the front pages of newspapers and in the news reels. He rose to greet me.

'Felix, lovely to meet you.' He gripped my hand firmly and pulled me towards him, leaving me in no doubt who was in control.

'Lord Burke, it's a pleasure to meet you.'

He grinned. 'Pleasure's all mine, Felix, I'm a huge fan.'

'You are?'

'Don't look so surprised, dear boy. I love the comedies of Shakespeare and, in my humble opinion, nobody plays them better than you.'

I glanced at Morris, who was nodding his approval.

'You're right, Leo,' said Morris. 'Felix has a gift for the lighter roles of lesser substance.' And there it was. Faint praise underscored by a subtle slur. Lord Burke didn't seem to notice though, he seemed genuinely pleased to meet me.

'You'll have to give me some tips, I'm playing Malvolio for the Taff's Well Players next month.'

'It would be my pleasure, Lord Burke.'

'Oh, call me Leo, please. We don't need such formality between us actors.'

I glanced across at Morris, over Leo's shoulder, and he winked at me. In that moment, everything became clear. Lord Leo Burke of Ponty, despite his huge worth, was a frustrated thespian. Morris had discovered this and used it to his advantage; courting Leo, befriending him and then drawing him to his inner circle.

This was how he would build his empire. He had the talent and the vision, he had a great team of actors around him and now he had the patronage of one of the most powerful industrialists in Europe to fund his plans.

All the pieces were in place. Sir Miles was dead and Richard was out of the picture, never to properly return, although we didn't know it back then.

He had one final performance left. If you had read the reviews by Terry Fibs and Gerard Soames the next day, you would have thought the performance was a disaster but, for me, and the audience in the theatre that night, it was the greatest performance they would ever see.

'Take a seat, gents, our other guests will be here soon.'

'Who else is joining us?'

'Two up-and-coming art critics, Terence Fibs and Gerard Soames.'

Leo nodded his approval. 'Oh yes, I met them at one of Ossie's dinner parties.'

'Ossie?' I asked.

'Oswald Moseley, fine fellow. Throws an excellent dinner party and the conversation is always interesting.'

'But he's a fascist!'

Leo smiled. 'Oh come, come now, Felix. One man's fascist is another man's freedom fighter, he's just misunderstood and often misquoted. I assume that's why he has taken Fibs and Soames under his wing. They work for papers that at least give him a fair crack of the whip.'

After listening to Leo defend Moseley, and mention Fibs and Soames as supporters, I had already formed the opinion that I would not like them. It was a sound opinion that time and events would prove well-founded.

I wanted to argue the point with regard to Moseley, but one glance at Morris' face made me hold my tongue. I sat there for the next few minutes making small talk and desperately wishing to be anywhere else but there. The arrival of Fibs and Soames, some minutes later, came as something of a relief. That relief proved to be temporary.

'Ah, here they are,' proclaimed Morris, rising from his chair as if greeting the second coming of the Lord. I stood to greet them. On first inspection, there didn't appear to be anything worth greeting. Fibs looked like a rat in a suit he had stolen from a mortuary, and Soames like a snake that had learned to stand upright. Although he walked, he gave the distinct impression that he slithered. I shuddered. Was this the price we had to pay to be successful?

'Lovely to meet you, Lord Burke, such a pleasure,' hissed Soames, his voice whistling the s of such and sounding to all the world, or to me, at least, of a constrictor that had taught itself to speak.

To his left, Fibs waited nervously for his moment, his ratty nose twitching as the waiter passed with the cheese board. I stifled laughter as I realised I was letting my instant dislike run away with my imagination.

'Nice to see you again.' His voice was high-pitched, conjuring the image of a rat from a children's nursery rhyme. Where was the Pied Piper when you needed him?

We all sat down as the drinks arrived and Morris got down to the nitty gritty.

'It's wonderful to have you all here for dinner at the inception of something that, I think we all agree, could be a gift for the ages. A new dynasty in British, nay, world theatre.' Morris had found his flow and his audience. It didn't take long for his master plan to emerge and it was worse than I could ever have imagined.

'Now, Leo,' we were all on first name terms by this stage, 'has agreed, because of his love of the arts, and Shakespeare in particular, to become the patron of the Morris Oxford Players. For which mere thanks can never be enough.'

Leo smiled effusively. 'It's my pleasure, Morris, anything one can do to help the arts and promote the Bard. I feel it's my civic and moral obligation to do so.'

I felt it was probably a good way for my new best friend, Leo, Lord Burke of Ponty, to wash some of his dirty cash from the shadier depths of his vast portfolio. I still hadn't worked out what the rodent and reptilian pressmen were doing there, but I was soon to discover.

Morris continued. 'With Leo's help we are going to reshape theatre, give Shakespeare the new adaptations that the texts cry out for, and, we could try some new material from contemporary writers that will reflect the turbulent world in which we are living. How does that sound?'

It sounded bloody awful to me but I held my tongue. Having seen two medium rare fillet steaks arrive at the next table, my moral outrage at being asked to sit down with potential fascists, reptilians and vermin was placated by the desire to bury my teeth in the carnivore's banquet that lay so invitingly beside us.

Morris then revealed his master plan. 'To become the pre-eminent theatre group in the country, we need several things in place. Great actors, we have those. A great patron, we have Leo. The final ingredient is the press. We need voices in the press that supply unflinching support at all times.'

There was an awkward silence, eventually broken by Fibs. 'How will that work? Critics have to be objective. It's the nature of the job.'

Morris pulled a face. 'Is it though, Terence? I always believed it was a critics job to give an opinion. All art is subjective and opinions may vary but, if your opinions vary in favour of our performances, there could be huge benefits.'

I couldn't believe what I was hearing. Was the great Morris Oxford in the process of trying to buy influence? Of course he was. But the way he did it? That, indeed, was something to behold.

'Let me get this straight, Morris,' said Gerard Soames, clearly as surprised as me but keeping his options wide open. 'You want us to give unerringly positive reviews ... Why would we do that?'

All eyes turned to Morris. 'The usual reason. Money!'

Fibs and Soames looked at each other, Morris' candour had caught them off guard. Soames spoke for them. 'You can't really think that we could be bought, surely?'

'A lot of money,' added Morris.

That made them pause. Soames looked at me. 'Are you comfortable with this, Felix?'

I shrugged, fearing any comment would implicate me.

Soames looked to Morris. 'Hardly a ringing endorsement, is it?'

'I don't think you understand what Morris is offering you,' said Leo. 'There is no bribery involved in this offer. I take it you have both been to performances that have been given by Morris and his players?' They both nodded. 'What did you think?'

'Quite wonderful,' hissed Soames.

'Outstanding,' squeaked Fibs.

'And there you have it,' said Leo, triumphantly. 'We all agree that Morris and his players are wonderful. All we are asking you to do is confirm this on a regular basis, through all your papers and radio interviews. Affirmation on a sustained basis is—'

'Propaganda?' I interrupted, unable to restrain my tongue any longer. Morris shot me a withering look but Leo, with the endless affability of vast wealth, smoothed the edges of my assertion.

'Yes, you could say that, but what do we mean by propaganda? For me, it implies a positive promotion of something where excellence lies, bringing it to the masses. Proclaiming to the world that here is something for the ages. If I was a young critic, I would want to be a part of that, especially for the inside line and the exclusivity that such a relationship would bring.'

With those few short words, Leo had clinched the deal and, from that time on, Terry Fibs and Gerard Soames would be the mouthpieces of the Morris Oxford Players; their glowing tributes bought by the forty pieces of gold that Lord Leo would place upon their palms.

Those reviews would also occasionally pick out certain actors for criticism. It was a weapon of control, delivered by Morris from the pens of his acolytes. It was a masterstroke. What actor ever had his own resident press corps that appeared, to all intents and purposes, to be entirely independent, objective even? This was empire building, the likes of which the theatre had never seen and would hopefully never see again, and I was there at the moment of its inception.

Chapter 11
Childhood's End

Morris had planned well; Desmond Tharpe and I were contracted for the next two seasons, as was Beatrice. Richard was on sick leave and not expected to return any time soon. Terry Fibs and Gerard Soames had become part of Morris' social circle and I, along with the rest of the Morris Oxford Players, was forced to see more of them than I would have cared to. Morris was creating his own publicity machine. It was clever, disturbingly so. As critics, they had everything but objectivity. This was a cult of personality; Morris Oxford's.

As the cast grew and our future was planned for one, two, sometimes three years ahead, I learned to ignore the nasty taste in my mouth. My reputation was growing, as was my income. At what point did I realise I had sold out? When I ignored a possible murder and looked the other way while Morris slept with my best friend's wife. Accepted roles that I knew should have been Richard's.

Truth be told, I knew from the very beginning. Success is a gilded cage; it's comfortable, well paid and good for your ego. It becomes easy to forget the things that really matter; emotions like humility, guilt and compassion. The line between right and wrong is redrawn. Self-interest creeps up on you until it controls your every action, your every thought. Soon you forget what you did to get here, forget the people you passed on the way and those you climbed over en route. Things were good and I was too busy to have regrets. Onwards and upwards, me, me, me! Until …

'Can I have a word, Felix?'

I turned around and there was Beatrice; she looked pale,

nervous. We hadn't spoken for some time. I hadn't told her why I had distanced myself from her, and being so close now felt uncomfortable. I still saw Richard on a regular basis, but he was so deep in his depression and drinking that talking to him was like trying to tune a radio. Every now and then something would come through loud and clear but then I would lose the signal and a veil of white noise would be drawn down, so nothing intelligible could be heard. He was almost out of reach, fading away like a dying star. I couldn't bear to look at Beatrice when I was with Richard, the betrayal was just too much, and yet, I stayed.

'Sure, what can I do for you, Beatie?'

'In private.' She looked worried, the glow of her natural beauty diminished.

I pointed towards the canteen. 'Fancy a cuppa? It'll be quiet in there now.'

She nodded. 'Yes, that would be lovely.'

We walked in silence down the corridor and up the stairs; two friends divided by the same secrets. Beatrice found a table in the far corner while I went and bought the teas. When I returned, she was wringing her hands nervously.

'What's on your mind, Beatie?'

She gazed into the steam that rose from her mug, lost in thought, reaching for the words to express what she wanted to say. When she looked up at me, she was no longer a woman, she looked like a child; small, helpless and consumed by guilt.

'I've done something stupid.'

I was about to berate her, reveal that I knew what she had done and how stupid it was. But, before I could get into my lecture, she said something that left the words stuck in my throat.

'I'm pregnant.'

My first thought was, is it Richard's? Somehow, I managed not to say it. 'Er, congratulations. How does Richard feel about it?'

Tears welled in her eyes. 'It's not his.'

I knew whose it was, I couldn't believe it. I should have made it easier for her but I didn't. 'Who's the father?'

She looked down at her steaming mug, slowly shaking her head. 'I'm sorry, Felix, so very sorry.'

She waited for me to respond; I was feeling vindictive and said nothing. I just waited for her to reveal the secret I already knew.

'It's Morris.'

And there it was, out in the open for all to see. The cuckolding of Richard was complete.

'Have you told Morris?'

'No.'

'Have you told Richard?'

She shook her head. 'I don't think he could take it.'

'Well maybe you should have thought of that before you threw yourself at Morris to get better parts.'

I hadn't meant to say it, it just came out. Secrets always come out. My words had the effect I had hoped for. Her mouth fell open and she looked like she had been electrocuted.

'That's not true.'

'It is, Beatrice, don't lie to me too. If you want to confide in me, do me the courtesy of telling the truth.' That was rich coming from me, but righteous indignation felt good.

'We just drifted in to an affair, it was never planned.'

'I heard you, Beatie, in the park that night. You told Morris if he gave you better parts you would sleep with him.'

'Oh.'

'So, don't tell me any more lies. What are you going to do?'

'I don't know.'

'Are you sure Morris is the father?'

She nodded. 'Richard and I haven't had sex in months.'

'And Morris is the only man you've had sex with apart from Richard?'

'Of course, what kind of a woman do you think I am!'

'We know what kind of woman you are, Beatie, I'm just checking on numbers.'

She leaned forward and slapped me hard. 'How dare you!'

'Richard's my friend.'

'But you don't seem to have any problem taking his parts.' She was right. Who was I to sit in judgement on anyone.

'I'm sorry. What are you going to do?'

She started to cry again. 'I don't know.' She looked lost. 'Everything's going wrong. Help me, Felix.'

I reached out and took her hand. 'You can't tell Richard, he's too fragile. Do you want Morris to know?'

'I don't know.'

I felt uncomfortable being cast in the role of advisor. 'You want some honest advice?' She nodded. 'Get rid of it.'

It was tough advice, too harsh. Beatrice had been raised Catholic and, despite her modern-girl lifestyle, old habits die hard.

'That would be a sin.'

I shrugged. 'Your choice, but if you tell Morris, he will drop you from the play. Think about it – in a few months, you won't be able to act in anything … For quite a while.'

'He wouldn't, he loves me.'

'He loves only what he sees in the mirror. What he has is lust, I don't think he is capable of love.'

'I won't get rid of my baby.'

'Well, tell Morris and, when he tries to drop you from the cast, you can threaten to reveal to everyone that he is the father. A blood test would be an easy way to prove it. Then you have him over a barrel, too.'

'Yes, that would work. I could tell Richard that the baby is his, it worked with Oliver.'

For a moment, I wasn't sure what I had heard. 'I'm sorry?'

'It worked with Oliver.'

The sickening truth was hard to digest; my little godson was not Richard's.

'Who's the father?' I didn't need to ask the question, I already knew. The overheard conversation in the park two months before came flooding back. Morris had said, 'You will come back to me?' Why hadn't I seen it before?

'You were lovers back then.'

'Yes. Morris seduced me, I was too easily swayed. I felt flattered by his attention. Richard and I weren't married then. When I became pregnant, I knew Morris would want to put a ring on my finger.'

'Why didn't you let him?'

'It was Richard I loved. You knew him back then, he was amazing. Crazy but brilliant. We all knew he had greatness in him, he was exciting to be around.'

'And Morris was just too boring?'

We both smiled and she nodded.

'Yes, he's always been boring. It's always been about the work and his career. He's a damn fine actor but he doesn't come close to Richard on a good day. Morris is just really good at self-promotion.'

An awkward silence fell between us. She had revealed so much that changed the way I viewed everything. If these secrets came out, our whole world would collapse.

'What are you going to do?'

She looked at me and it told me all I needed to know. 'I know somebody who had an abortion, a private doctor in Cheltenham sorted it. You want me to get his details?'

'Abortion, it's such an ugly word. Do you think I should?'

'Only you can answer that, Beatie. In your place, I think I would. If you don't and this comes out, you'll lose Richard, your career, and the press will have a field day with you and Morris. It doesn't bear thinking about.'

She nodded. 'You're right. Will you come with me? I can't do it on my own.'

I moved over and hugged her. 'Of course I will.'

I could feel her trembling in my arms, like a frightened little bird, and I felt more helpless than I had ever been. The people I loved were sinking into a mire of their own making and I wasn't sure that I could pull them out.

A few days later, we made the call. Two weeks after that, we made the trip to Cheltenham. The journey back to Stratford passed in almost total silence, what could we say? A terrible situation had been avoided but it had only masked the problem. Beneath the surface of our privileged lives there was a cancer, undiagnosed and spreading.

Two weeks later, Morris and I were finishing some special additional rehearsal scenes for *Dream*. He had a couple of bits of business he wanted to work into a scene. He was not comfortable with comedy so he would always try to work in some comedic interludes to lighten the mood and get a laugh. Richard wouldn't have had to do it but Morris did, and the fact that he did made his well-rehearsed spontaneity look natural. Morris was good, but only because he went the extra mile.

Perhaps that's what defines greatness; the willingness to do whatever it takes to succeed. Helping Sir Miles into heaven a little sooner than planned was one thing, pushing Richard over the edge was another. Morris was driven and ruthless. It was starting to look like a winning combination.

Chapter 12
The Closing of the Ranks

Valentine Parks was a pretentious prat; he was also the artistic director at the theatre. He watched over proceedings like a hawk, offering his opinion on everything. You knew you had a problem if he was watching rehearsal, then held up his hand and uttered *those* words.

'It's wonderful, darling … but …'

That line had ruined many a rehearsal. Morris and I were going through Act 1, Scene 3 from *Macbeth*, where Macbeth and Banquo meet the three witches in foul weather. Morris was trying to hone the scene but we didn't have our actresses around so he had roped in three set builders to read in their places. They were a bit wooden, which was to be expected of carpenters, but it enabled Morris and I to perform our parts.

Macbeth   'So foul and fair a day I have not seen.'
Banquo   'How far is't called to Forres?'
            (*The three set builders step forward, all in jeans and T-shirts.*)

            'What are these
            So withered and so wild in their attire?'

Morris started to snigger but I pressed on.

            'They look not like inhabitants of the earth, and yet are on it?' (*To the Witches*)
            'Are you living?'

'Who can tell? He's from Wellesbourne,' said Morris.

'Wellesbourne is famous for its great beauties,' said Harry.

'Really?'

Harry shrugged. 'Nah, I just made that up.'

We all laughed and then we pressed on.

Macbeth	'Speak, if you can. What are you?'
First Witch	'All hail, Macbeth! Hail to thee, Thane of Glamis!'
Second Witch	'All hail, Macbeth! Hail to thee, Thane of Cawdor!'
Third Witch	'All hail, Macbeth! That shalt be king hereafter!'

'Well! It's absolutely marvellous, but … What the hell is going on?'

I turned around to see poor Valentine looking totally confused. I was about to respond but, for once, I was beaten to the punch by Morris ad-libbing.

'The people's theatre, Valentine. We take local people and put them on the stage in minor roles.'

'Over my dead body, you will.'

Morris and I looked at each other.

'My brother's an undertaker in Stratford, he could do you a deal.'

Valentine shot him a withering look. 'I know your brother. Cold hands. He's not packing me off to the hereafter.'

'It'll be pretty warm where you're going, Val.'

'Be that as it may, Morris, you can't be dragging in set builders to fill your cast. This is Stratford, we have standards to maintain.'

'But Harry makes a very convincing witch.'

'And I can make my own broomstick,' said Harry.

'No, no, no! I don't know where you got this idea for people's theatre but this isn't Russia, we don't do communism here. This theatre isn't for the people, it's for the elite.' Valentine turned to the three carpenters. 'No offense, gents, but none of you are attractive enough to play witches.'

Harry the Hammer looked genuinely hurt. 'I was channelling

Cybil Thorndike.'

'I thought you captured the emotion of the part very nicely,' said Plywood Pete.

'It's not easy being in character wearing working clothes.'

'Enough,' bellowed Valentine. 'This is not going to happen, do you understand?'

Morris winked at the three carpenters and they all started laughing. Valentine soon cottoned on that he'd been had and joined in but, behind his smile, I saw resentment. He had made a note of this, and Morris and I definitely had a black mark on our records. Looking back, Valentine wasn't a bad artistic director, his real problem was that he was rooted to tradition. This was the thirties; actors and directors the world over were trying new interpretations of Shakespeare that reflected the world we now lived in. Valentine's idea of an interpretation was to change the colour of Malvolio's crossed garters, hardly a groundbreaking move.

"Say the lines and don't bump into the furniture," was his only instruction.

This suited Morris well, he was old school too. He possessed a magnificent voice, full of emotion and controlled power. When he spoke, you listened, and that was my criticism of him. When you had a scene with him, he would say his lines and then wait for his next turn. He never seemed engaged with what the actor opposite was saying. That was just a gap until his next line. There was no real emotional engagement, which is probably why he rarely had any film or TV work. His performances were too big, declamatory. But nobody could deliver a soliloquy like Morris and that guaranteed his success. He'd tried his hand at TV but he never managed to dial it back; instead of just performing to a person behind the camera, he was still playing to a full theatre.

Richard's style of acting could not have been more different. When you acted with him, you forgot the audience, it was as if we were the only people in the world. Sometimes he would draw me in so deeply, I could hardly remember my lines. He was different every night too, always finding something new to tap into, his character constantly evolving.

This total immersion in character took its toll. At the end of each play, he was totally spent, having experienced every emotion that his character called for. You could see the price he paid for such intensity but, while it lasted, it was mesmerising.

'Don't you want to try something different?' asked Morris.

'Something different? I don't like the sound of that. Shakespeare wrote it the way he wanted it performed, let's not mess with it.'

'I would never mess with the text, Val, you know that. I just wanted to try some business out. I think the reaction between Macbeth and Banquo in this scene could get a good laugh if we time the lines, throw in a pause and exchange a look.'

Valentine didn't seem convinced. 'Which lines?'

'What are these, so withered, and so wild in their attire. I look to Banquo, who looks at them and shrugs, while the three witches look offended.'

Valentine nodded. 'Yes, that could work.'

'Oh, it will,' enthused Morris. 'Imagine the reaction we could get from, Speak if you can. What are you?'

'It's a cheap laugh, but viable.'

Morris hid his irritation at Valentine's put down.

'It breaks the tension for a moment before we plunge in to the prediction. If Felix and I can get the rhythm right, it could be a winner.'

'If you must, just make sure you don't mess with the text.' Valentine turned on his heel and left, no smile and no goodbye.

That was the nature of the man; he would cruise around the theatre, giving everyone the benefit of his wisdom, whether they wanted it or not, and then, like the ghost of King Hamlet, disappear into the mist.

'How old do you think Valentine is?' asked Morris.

'Hard to say, he's always looked old. Seventy-something?'

Morris nodded. 'Yeah, still, he'll soon be dead.' A broad smile spread across his face. 'I hope I get to do his eulogy, guess how I'll start it?'

'Finally?'

He laughed. 'That would be good, but that's not it.' Morris stepped dramatically forward and held up his right hand. 'His life was wonderful … but!'

Even the three witches laughed.

Morris now had the control he desired: his own critics and the patronage of one of the wealthiest men in Europe. He led the company, picked his roles and, for the most part, was left alone by Valentine and the rest of the management. This was the start of his empire, one that would last for decades. He drew his players around him, closing ranks to all who would threaten his control, limit his horizons. The only threat to his pre-eminence had been Richard, and we all waited to see if he would ever get back to the actor he had once been.

Two nights later, I went to see him. Beatrice had told me she was going out and wanted me to pop round; Richard would be there babysitting young Oliver. When I reached the little terraced house on Ryland Street, I knocked on the door, unsure of what would greet me. There was no reply. I knocked again and waited. Nothing. I was about to turn and leave when I decided to try the door. It was open. I stepped into the hallway.

'Hello? You there, Richard?' I heard a movement from the kitchen. 'Hi Rich, it's Felix.'

I heard a grunt. I couldn't decipher any meaning but I took it as a greeting. When I pushed open the door, I barely recognised the face that looked up at me. Richard had aged; his face was drawn, gaunt. He was like a little old man, how could someone age so quickly? All the coiled energy that had made him so dangerous, so vital, seemed to have seeped away.

'Hello, Felix. Don't get too close, failure is contagious.' He tried to make a joke of it but it was just too sad to be funny.

'How are you feeling?'

He thought about it for a moment. 'I don't know. Bad, I think.'

'You're looking better.'

He laughed without humour. 'For an actor, you're a terrible liar. I look like I died two weeks ago and they dug me up just to be sure I was dead. Lazarus, without the happy ending, if you will.'

I tried to smile but it was hard, my friend was disappearing before my eyes.

'Can't wait to get you back on stage, mate, it's not the same without you.'

He looked right through me, his eyes fixed on something that only he could see.

'Not sure I'll be coming back, Felix. Can't seem to find the motivation. Morris doesn't want me.'

'He's frightened of the competition.'

'He may well be but he's managed to sideline me. Not sure I'll ever get a decent role here again. Not while he's in charge.'

'Go back to Bristol.'

He shook his head. 'I think I've burned my bridges there, they never wanted me to leave and coming back here really threw dirt in their faces.'

He was right. Bristol Old Vic had coaxed him away from Stratford on the understanding that he would stay for at least two seasons, they wanted to build a new company around him. Returning to Stratford after just one show seemed like a betrayal, especially after the reviews had mentioned that this could be "the beginnings of a dynasty".

'I have a mate at the Birmingham Rep; you want me to have a word?'

He shook his head. 'Thanks, but I really don't think I'd be any good right now. I feel like I'm standing on a stage and the curtain is down and it won't open. I can hear the crowd but I just can't get to them.'

As a metaphor, it captured his situation perfectly. I felt I was on the other side of that curtain and couldn't get through to him. He was there but not there, elusive, like a memory that was incomplete. How do you reach someone who has lost themselves?

'How's little Oliver?'

For a moment, his face brightened. 'Oh, Oliver is wonderful! If it wasn't for him and Beatie, I don't think I could go on. That boy is the light of my life; being his father is the only thing that really means anything.'

His words were like little stab wounds in my heart. How could I tell him he was living a lie? That Oliver was not his son and Morris was having some sort of affair with his wife? He could never be allowed to find out, he just wouldn't be able to cope.

Secrets, damn secrets. Insidious, poisoning everything that was good and destroying the future we had all once thought was our right. At that moment, I wasn't sure that I could ever be happy again.

Chapter 13
A Gilded Cage

The first night of *Dream* was upon us. The weeks of rehearsal had not been wasted; the show was slick and funny. Beatrice had received the reward for the wages of her sin and had been granted the starring role she craved, but not the one she expected.

In a rare moment of experimentation, Morris had made the bold decision to make Puck female and cast Beatrice in the role. This was entirely unexpected. Puck was very much viewed as a male role but, occasionally, had been played by a female. It was a part which lent itself to interpretation.

Valentine had gone into orbit when he saw it in dress rehearsal. 'Jesus H Christ, man, what the hell do you think you are doing? Puck is a man.'

'Is he though?' questioned Morris.

'Of bloody course he is. It says so in the text. He's referred to using male pronouns throughout the play.'

Morris nodded. 'I know but—'

'There is no but,' snapped Valentine, who looked like he was at bursting point. 'Would you play Juliet as a horse?'

'No,' said Morris. 'That wouldn't make sense, a horse wouldn't be able to pick up Romeo's dagger and stab itself.'

Valentine looked at Morris as if he had gone mad. 'You're taking me too literally.'

Morris paid no heed to Valentine's protest. 'Romeo wouldn't have been too pleased, can you imagine.'

'"But soft, what light through yonder window breaks? It is the East, and Juliet is" a … horse?'

The whole cast started to laugh, even the crew joined in.

Valentine remained unmoved. 'I will not accept Puck as a

woman.'

Morris stood his ground. 'Tough, that's the way we have rehearsed it and that's the way it's staying.'

It was open defiance. The theatre fell silent as we all waited for the explosion from Valentine which never came. His face darkened as his rage consumed him but he kept it in check, he knew that it was too late to make changes now.

When he spoke, his voice was cold, calm and dangerous. 'Very well, Morris. Have your little experiment but, make no mistake, when it goes wrong, the world will know it was your idea because I will tell them.'

Morris shrugged. 'Fair enough, Val.'

'Is that all you have to say on the matter?'

'I think it is. This is the best way to play it, Beatrice is amazing.'

Morris turned out to be right. Beatrice's portrayal of Puck was groundbreaking. She morphed between the sexes; at one moment all subtle, sly femininity, the next full of male bravado. Her performance was immense, that was its tragedy, it was too good.

At the end of the first night, the crowd went wild. When Beatrice came down to take her curtain call, her applause rose to a crescendo which left Morris standing at the back of the stage. As she took her bows it continued, unabated. I watched Morris' pleasure slowly fade away. Beatrice's applause was going on a bit.

Finally, when there was no sign of it dying down, Morris walked down to the front of the stage for his acclaim. It was good, but not as loud or long as Beatrice's. He tried to hide it but I could see that he was irritated.

He had created a star, one that had, on this night, outshone him. There was nothing he could do now; the die was cast. Beatrice would take centre stage until the end of the show's run, but he had already decided that Beatrice Smallman had played her last comedic role. She was too good at it, what was the point of sidelining Richard if his wife stepped into his challengers' shoes?

They may be lovers but they would not be co-stars. He knew she struggled to play serious roles and, from that point on, those were the only roles he would cast her in. When she won a London Critic's award at the end of the year and he didn't, it put the final nail in her career coffin. From that point on, she was destined to be outacted by the scenery as she struggled to play the tragic roles that were just not her *métier*.

It was a terrible thing for Morris to do; sabotage the career of the woman he purported to love. This was his tragedy, an ego so insecure, attached to an ambition that knew no bounds. Anything, or anyone, that stood in its way would be trampled underfoot.

The final realisation of this was still in the future. For now, we rode the acclaim and the applause that seemed our right. We were happy, even I was happy. But those secrets, like a cancer, were eating away at the very foundation of our joy. Everything was built on sand, and very soon those sands would shift and, in that shift, great tectonic plates would open and one of our number would disappear into the void.

Secrets, secrets, they will always find you out.

Chapter 14
Storm Clouds Gathering

'This is not going to end well,' said Morris, putting down his paper.

I looked up from my diary. 'What's not going to end well?'

'The Germans, Felix. Don't you read the papers?'

'No, far too depressing these days.'

'Well, belt up, old son, it's about to get worse. With the Germans back in the Rhineland that mad man Hitler will never stop.'

'He's just a windbag who likes to dress up in fancy outfits, nobody takes him seriously.'

With hindsight, I realise that Morris had looked at me with the contempt my remarks deserved.

He picked up his pipe and lit it. 'Mark my words, Felix, he won't stop. Before this decade is out the whole of Europe will be at war, and you know what that means.'

'No holidays in the south of France,' I suggested.

'No, conscription. You and I, and all other eligible men of age, will be forced to join the forces to fight.'

I wasn't so sure. 'Do you really think it will come to that?'

'I do,' he confirmed. 'The theatre will close and all of this will come to an end, for us anyway. The older actors may carry it on while we are away, but what if we don't return?'

'You're serious, aren't you.'

'Deadly,' said Morris. 'Nobody's tried to stop him, next it will be Austria and then the Sudetenland. Who knows where it will end?'

His concern gave me pause for thought. 'Well, if we do get the call, what can we do?'

'We can fight.'

'I took that as a given,' I said.

'No. Fight to stay at the theatre. We must think of the people, they need their theatre to keep them entertained.'

This was classic Morris. As a world war threatened, his only thought was how he could keep acting, stay on the stage. The real world was just a backdrop for him.

I tried to laugh the threat off. 'It may never happen, Morris, let's worry about it when the time comes.'

'That's typical of you, Felix, never planning for the future. You always need a plan. I have a plan, a back-up plan and a back-up for the back-up plan.'

'Is that all? You're leaving a lot to chance. Let's plan our war contingency, just in case.'

'Good idea, Felix. I'll grab my notebook.'

He hurried from the room in search of his book and I just shook my head. Morris *would* be great one day, because he was totally focused on one thing; himself.

As the run of *Dream* neared its end, our thoughts shifted to the next play on our books: *Othello*. I was looking forward to this. Morris had cast me as Iago; evil, cunning and two-faced, he was a terrible person and they were always the best parts to play.

Beatrice was cast as Ophelia and she wasn't happy. 'I really don't want this role, Felix, it's just not me.'

'You'll be great, look at your reviews for *Dream*. You're a star now.'

'In comedy. I can't do tragedy, it's too dark.'

She was right, of course. I had seen her struggle with such roles in *Hamlet* and *Richard III*. She had a lightness of touch that worked so well in comedy, but could not be transferred to the darker roles, so she suffered. She overacted terribly. She begged Morris not to cast her, but he wouldn't take no for an answer. He knew that she would fail and he wanted, needed, her to.. There was only room for one star in his company and it wasn't going to be Beatrice.

While we were talking, young Oliver came into the room. He was nearly four.

'Uncle Felix,' he cried with delight, then ran over and jumped onto my lap.

'Hello, Oliver, how are you?'

'I'm sad.' He looked up at me with puffy eyes.

'Why are you sad?'

He looked across to Beatrice, as if seeking her permission to tell me, and then turned back to me. 'Daddy isn't very well, he's been crying.'

I looked over at Beatrice and she nodded faintly, confirming Oliver's story.

'And why is Daddy so sad?'

'Because Uncle Morris hates him.'

It was a shocking thing to hear from the mouth of a four-year-old, and Beatrice interrupted.

'You can't say that, Oliver. It's not fair to Uncle Morris.'

It was, and she knew it, but you really can't let a young child think like that.

'I don't think he does; Uncle Morris is Daddy's friend.'

'Then why does he make him cry?'

I didn't really have an answer to that, not even a lie.

'Don't bother Uncle Felix with that now, Oliver. Why don't you do your Hamlet speech.'

Oliver's eyes brightened. 'Can I, Mummy?'

'Of course, darling. Uncle Felix would love to hear it, wouldn't you?'

I was a little taken aback. I knew Oliver was a precocious young fellow, but Hamlet was a big ask for a four-year-old. I fixed my smile and prepared for the worst. 'I'd love to hear your Hamlet, Oliver. Which speech are you doing?'

'I have of late,' he stated, offering no further explanation.

'Wow, that's a serious speech for a young man.'

For the first time that day, I saw Beatrice smile. 'Give him a chance, Felix, I think you'll be impressed.'

I sat back and braced myself, but Oliver was about to prove me wrong. He walked to the middle of the room, looked down at the floor and took a couple of deep breaths. When he looked up, his face was no longer that of a child, but a confused and conflicted teenager. The transformation was remarkable. And then, he began.

"'I have of late, but wherefore I know not, lost all my mirth, forgone all custom of exercises, and, indeed, it goes so heavily with my disposition that this goodly frame, the Earth, seems to me a sterile promontory; this most excellent canopy, the air, look you, this brave o'er hanging firmament, this majestical roof, fretted with golden fire—why, it appeareth nothing to me but a foul and pestilent congregation of vapours.'"

I was dumbstruck. This young boy was bringing an emotional intensity to Shakespeare's words that even I would struggle to match. It was almost surreal; I was being moved to tears by his performance, as was he. I could see the sorrow in his features. I glanced across at Beatrice and she smiled knowingly, she was sharing her secret with me. Oliver was a child prodigy.

"'What a piece of work is a man, how noble in reason, how infinite in faculties, in form and moving how express and admirable; in action how like an angel, in apprehension how like a god: the beauty of the world, the paragon of animals—and yet to me, what is this quintessence of dust? Man delights not me, no, nor women neither, though by your smiling you seem to say so.'"

It was breathtaking. Oliver had imbued the Bard's words with a depth of emotional understanding that just shouldn't be possible for a four-year-old, and yet I had just seen it with my own eyes. I started to applaud.

'Bravo, Oliver, that was amazing. How on earth did you learn that speech?'

'Daddy tells them to me at bedtime. He's even better than me.'

I looked at Beatrice and she nodded. 'Amazing, isn't he.'

'He really is. If I hadn't seen it with my own eyes, I wouldn't have believed it. He has his father's gift.'

The words were out of my mouth before I'd realised what I had said. Richard wasn't his father; Morris was.

The look on Beatrice's face spoke volumes; the guilt, the weight of the secrets, all of these were her burden to carry, and yet, Oliver was growing up to be a wonderful young man.

'Can I go now, Mummy? I want to play with Simon.'

In a moment, Oliver had snapped from being Hamlet, an emotionally ravaged young man, to an innocent young child keen to be outside with his friend.

'Of course, but stay in the garden, you know the rules.'

Oliver spun on his heels and hurried from the room, calling back over his shoulder as he did so. 'Bye, Uncle Felix. Love you.'

We listened to his footsteps disappearing down the hallway until we heard the back door to the garden close, leaving us alone to ponder the events that had created this situation.

'You can never tell Morris, he would use it to break Richard.'

Beatrice looked shocked. 'Morris would never do that. There would be too much bad press, he couldn't bear that.'

'I'm not so sure. He resents Richard's talent and I don't think he could keep the secret. It would come out one day.'

'I have no intention of it coming out. It's our secret, Felix. You're the only one I trust enough to share this with. I've been carrying this for four years. Getting pregnant with Morris' child was a mistake, a brief fling when Richard and I were having a tough time.'

'We all make mistakes, Beatrice.'

'Oliver wasn't a mistake, he's the best thing that's ever happened to me.'

'Sorry, bad choice of words. Oliver is wonderful, but what if he has to have a blood test or an operation one day? These things have a habit of coming out, it's not something you can bury forever.'

Beatrice looked lost. 'I know. I dread the day but, until then, I just have to carry on. When it comes out, everything will be ruined. Richard's trust in me, Morris' desire to own me and take Oliver under his wing. He would claim him as his own in a moment if he knew the truth.'

'So, what are you going to do?'

'Nothing. It's all I can do. Just keep going, waiting for the axe to fall.'

It was a terrible cloud under which to try and live a life. A cloud which would one day burst and drown her.

'Have you thought about how this would affect Richard?'

'I've thought of nothing else for four years.'

'You have to tell him.'

She looked at me, the fear in her eyes palpable. 'He can never know, it would kill him.'

'Not now, maybe when he is stronger, in a better place.'

'He's never going to be in a better place, it's not in his nature. Richard feels everything, the pain of the world sits on his shoulders like a weight. He doesn't have it in him to be truly happy, he just seems to absorb sorrow wherever he finds it. Maybe that's what makes him such a great actor.'

I couldn't argue with her. Richard was constantly disappointed by the world around him. He was always searching for hope and the world in 1936 was not an optimistic place; war was coming and we all knew it.

'So, we just go on and hope for the best?'

'Unless he dies.' She spoke the words so matter-of-factly that, for a moment, they didn't register with me.

'Sorry, is Richard ill?'

'He's having a mental breakdown, Felix, of course he's ill.'

'But it's not life threatening.'

'Hopefully not, but mental illness is a strange thing. One day he seems back to his old self, then the next day he is in a pit of despair. It's on those days that he talks about death.'

'Is he seeing somebody?'

She shook her head. 'No, I've tried but he refuses to go and see the doctor. I spoke to Dr Butts.'

'Oh, Henry is a great doctor, he'll sort him out.'

'He tried. He even found a psychiatrist in Leamington for Richard, but when I told him he went mad, ironically.'

'How mad?'

'Berserk. He was screaming that he didn't need to see a head doctor, there's nothing wrong with him. He was throwing things around the room. There was no reasoning with him. When he's like that, you can't talk to him. I sometimes think life would be better if he did kill himself.'

I was shocked. 'You can't mean that, Beatrice. It's Richard.'

'Oh, it's easy for you, Felix, you're just his friend. You come here and have a chat over a cuppa, say a few comforting words and then bugger off and get on with your life. It's not the same for me. I'm living this nightmare twenty-four hours a day. It's a life sentence with no parole.'

I hadn't understood what a burden Richard's illness had become for her but … to wish him dead? It was shocking. 'Isn't there anything else we can do?'

It was a stupid question. If he wouldn't even go to the doctor, he was never going to accept anything more intrusive. Richard had withdrawn deeply into himself, so deep that I could only see an occasional glimpse of the man I had loved like a brother for so many years.

I sat across from Beatrice in silence, I had no words. Sometimes events just overcome you. Richard's illness was one thing but the secrets that were piled up on top of it … I wasn't sure how Beatrice was managing to get out of bed in the morning. This whole situation was becoming unbearable. Something had to break. All we could do was cross our fingers and hope for the best. That was never going to work.

Chapter 15
We Few, We Happy Few

As autumn turned to winter, *Othello* began its run and reviews were good. Even I got some mentions for my Iago.

"Felix Richards oozes menace, hidden beneath an oily charm. He leaves the audience in no doubt that this Iago is a dark force. A disingenuous presence that is constantly plotting his friend's demise. It is a fine performance and marks the arrival of Felix Richards as a major talent."

Unsurprisingly, this didn't sit well with Morris. He had read the review and his only comment was, "Nice review, Felix. Only made possible by my vulnerability as Othello, of course."

And then he just walked off, as if that was a perfectly natural way to congratulate a fellow actor. Implying all of my success was down to him.

"Thank you, Morris, I couldn't have done it without you."

"I know," was all he replied, the words thrown over his shoulder as he walked away.

There were moments when Morris Oxford could be an absolute ass; they started when he woke up in the morning and ended when he went to sleep at night. I can't speak for his dreams but I'm pretty sure that he only ever dreamed about himself.

That season held one final tribute to be placed on the altar of Richard Jenkins' career. The production of *Othello* was alternating with *Henry V* and, naturally, Morris was playing Othello *and* Henry.

To be fair, he made an excellent King Hal; all big declamatory speeches and bravado. I had noticed, during a performance of *Othello*, that Morris' voice had begun to sound hoarse. This was unheard of, Morris' voice had never let him down. On this occasion, he'd barely managed to get to the end of the performance and, when he did, his voice was gone. A doctor was called and it was diagnosed as a throat strain. This should never have happened but Morris had decided that he wanted to play him with a north west African accent. 'He's a Moor, he must speak as a Moor,' was all Morris would say when I challenged him regarding the accent.

'You sound more like Al Jolson than Othello.'

There had been no discussing it after that exchange. Morris was determined to sound like a Moor, despite the fact he was a white man wearing black face. The irony of it seemed lost on him, as it was with many of us back then. The specialist diagnosed that the mangling of his vowels to get the accent had strained the muscles in his throat and they had gone into total spasm. It could take a day, maybe three, before it would recover; he would not be able to go on that night.

This presented a real problem. Desmond Tharpe was the understudy, but he had been allowed to take a week off in France to help his father move back to England. Unlike P. G. Wodehouse, Desmond's Father had no desire to become a prisoner of the Germans when they invaded. Most of the free world now thought that this could happen in the near future, if only the French military leaders had taken it as seriously as Desmond's father.

I digress. Without Desmond, we had no Henry.

Valentine was having a fit. 'What can we do? The house is sold out tonight. We can't refund all that money, it would be a tragedy.'

I looked around. No one had an answer and, for once, Morris had nothing to say. Robbed of his speech, he held up his hands as if admitting defeat. The whole company just stood there, helpless.

'What about Richard?'

My question took everyone by surprise. Morris' eyes bulged in protest but he remained silent. When the murmurings of the company failed to bring an objection, I continued.

'When he played Henry, at the Bristol Old Vic, it was acclaimed. I saw it. He was amazing. Why don't I ask him?'

Valentine thought about it for a moment. 'You think he could pull it off?'

'The role? No problem. As to whether he is physically able to handle the whole play, who knows … What choice do we have?'

Valentine was thinking hard. 'It could work. If he fails to finish the play, we can say he took ill during the performance. As long as the play starts, we won't have to give any refunds. Act of God and all that.'

I had to smile. Valentine, as always, was watching the bottom line and looking after the best interests of the theatre.

'Let me go and see him, Val. If I think he's up to it, I'll ask.'

'No, tell him he's on,' insisted Val.

I shook my head. 'No, I'll see how he is first. Give me an hour.'

When I reached Richard's house, I knocked and went straight in. 'Richard? Rich? It's Felix, where are you?'

'Looking down on you, as always,' came his voice from the top of the stairs.

I looked up. The sight that greeted me made my voice catch in my throat. 'Bloody hell, Rich, you've lost even more weight.'

He shrugged. 'Girth is overrated. What do you want, Felix?'

There was something about the way he had joked about his weight, a swagger in his delivery. Despite everything he had lost, was losing, it was still there. That indefinable quality that separated him from the rest of us.

'You want to play Henry tonight?' I made no preamble, what was the point? He could only say yes or no. As usual, I was wrong.

'Why?'

'Because Morris has lost his voice and Desmond is in France.'

A smile slowly spread across his face and he nodded. 'Once more unto the breach, dear friends.' The die was cast.

I, and the rest of the audience who witnessed Richard's performance that night will never forget it. It will live on in legend; in the memory of those who were actually there, and in the stories of those who said they were. If all who claimed to have been there were in attendance, ten thousand seats would not have been enough.

That night, we witnessed an amazing transformation; a broken man, lost and cast adrift by a sea of troubles, found himself on that stage. Became a King Henry like no other. He moved around the stage like a tiger, lithe and sinuous in movement, compelling and commanding in speech. He was the King, good King Hal, but he was *Richard's* King. His voice was strong and he sang the words like a confirmation of destiny, for this night Richard was himself. There was no disguising the lyrical Welsh tones of his voice, gone was the received pronunciation, the English that was expected. This night, King Hal was Welsh and it was wonderful.

I stood in the wings without moving, spellbound by what I was witnessing, knowing that if I lived to be a hundred I would never see its like again. Time has proven me right in that assumption. It was, quite simply, the greatest Henry ever seen.

At the curtain, I turned to the person standing next to me and realised that it was Morris, he had been there the whole time. Tears streamed down his face and he trembled with emotion. He slowly shook his head in awed disbelief. He could not speak but that did not matter, there was nothing to be said. There are moments in the theatre which surpass the ability of words to encompass and encapsulate the emotional depth of what you have witnessed. This was such a moment.

"Be in their flowing cups freshly remember'd.
This story shall the good man teach his son,
And Crispin Crispian shall ne'er go by,
From this day to the ending of the world,
But we in it shall be remember'd—
We few, we happy few, we band of brothers;
For he today that sheds his blood with me
Shall be my brother; be he ne'er so vile,
This day shall gentle his condition;
And gentlemen in England now abed
Shall think themselves accursed they were not here,
And hold their manhoods cheap whiles any speaks
That fought with us upon Saint Crispin's day."

I was there upon that day and, from that day until the ending of the world, he will be remembered. He was my brother. King Richard Jenkins.

Chapter 16
Farewell, Sweet Prince

The next morning, the town was abuzz with chatter about Richard's Henry; there was a genuine excitement amongst the cast. Morris was still silent, thanks to his damaged throat. The emotional depth of Richard's performance had moved him so deeply that he had instructed, in writing, I assume, Fibs and Soames to spread the word before their reviews were published. They had christened Richard's King "Llewellyn V". It had Morris' signature all over it. The man would stop at nothing to undermine anyone he viewed as his competition. It was a terrible thing to do but I had comforted myself with the look on Richard's face when I'd greeted him after the performance. He'd wrapped me in a huge hug, then pulled back and looked into my eyes.

'I showed them, Felix, I showed them.'

'You did, my friend. That was so honest, so beautiful.'

His smile slowly faded, and he whispered, 'That was all I ever wanted to do. Be me, up there. Not a version of me that they want, the real me, the Welsh me. I showed them.'

I watched him walk away down the corridor, towards his dressing room and, as he did, he seemed to shrink before my eyes. It seemed as if the king he had inhabited for the last three hours was leaving him, never to return. All that remained was a confused and diminished man. Without a script, he didn't know who he was any more.

The next day, I went to see Richard. I didn't realise that it would be the last time. A dark veil was draped across the sky, nature's curtain coming down. Heavy clouds filled the horizon making everything appear grey, all the vibrant colour of the summer now a faded memory. I hated winter and, on this day, the greyness was oppressive. Beatrice had asked me to sit with Richard while she took Oliver for a piano lesson. Not only was he a great little actor, it seemed he had a talent for music as well.

Beatrice had left the front door unlocked, you could do that in Stratford back then. As I entered the hallway, I called out to Richard but there was no reply. I checked the lounge and the kitchen – nothing. With a heavy heart, I made my way up the stairs. If he hadn't even managed to get out of bed, it didn't bode well. As I entered his bedroom, my worst fears were confirmed.

The blankets were scattered on the floor and Richard lay in the foetal position, shivering. He was muttering something under his breath, a constant chant that seemed familiar. I sat down on the bed and touched his shoulder. He didn't react. I listened harder to his muttering and, slowly, it began to make sense.

'To die, to sleep … What dreams may come. The heartache, the heartache and the thousand natural shocks that flesh is air to. To die, to sleep, tis a consummation to be wished. Dreams, what dreams.'

I recognised it, the *To be or not to be* speech from Hamlet. In his tormented dream state, the lines were all mixed up and repeated. It was disturbing to watch and listen to. Could this be the same man who, only last night, bestrode the stage like a colossus?

I tried to wake him by gently shaking his shoulder. 'Richard, it's Felix.'

His head turned towards me but his eyes remained closed. 'The sleep of death, death, dreams … What dreams may come.'

I tried again. 'Richard, wake up, it's Felix.'

Without warning, his eyes shot wide open, his body stiffened and he looked up at me with a haunted desperation I will never forget. 'Slings and arrows, Felix, slings and arrows. A sea of troubles, deep and dark, should I take arms against it. Sleep no more, sleep no more, sleep no more.'

He sat up and grabbed my elbow with a strength so unexpected it made me wince.

'For in that sleep of death, what dreams may come. When we have shuffled off this mortal coil, the heartache, devoutly to be wished. This makes a calamity of so long a life.'

I looked into his eyes and could not find the man I knew, but he was in there somewhere. Hidden behind a closed door that I couldn't find the key to. I had never felt more helpless or wretched in my life. I had heard him do that speech so many times and every time it had been breathtaking. This time, despite the jumbled repetition of the text, there were still moments that made the hairs on the back of my neck stand on end. He slumped back down on the bed, seemingly spent by the effort.

I gently stroked his head. His eyes opened again and he spoke, this time clearly and without confusion.

'The undiscovered country from whose bourn
No traveller returns, puzzles the will
And makes us rather bear those ills we have
Than fly to others that we know not of?'

He paused for a moment, and then continued.

'The fair Ophelia—Nymph, in thy orisons
Be all my sins remembered. All my sins!'

It felt like he was saying goodbye. I covered him with the sheets and sat with him for another hour, talking to him about our many great days upon the stage. I told him how amazing his performance of Henry had been. I asked him how his son was, feeling, as I did so, like a traitor. The secrets that I held strangled me with guilt, even though I had done nothing wrong; just the knowledge of this betrayal haunted me. If he ever emerged from the pit of despair he was now drowning in, discovering those hidden truths would send him plunging back down.

There were tears in my eyes when I heard the front door open. I leaned down and kissed him on the cheek. 'Now cracks a noble heart. Good night, sweet prince, and flights of angels sing thee to thy rest.'

When I closed the bedroom door behind me, I had a terrible feeling that we would never speak again; that the closing of it was an ending. Everything we had done, and been, was left behind. That undiscovered country, from whose bourn no traveller returns. He was gone, on a journey that he must take alone. A place where no love or friendship could reach.

I hurried down the stairs, tears streaming down my face. Beatrice looked up at me, her expression pained, but said nothing. This seemed like an ending and there were no words to soften that blow.

When I got back to the theatre, I found Morris in his office. He held up a hand to indicate that he still couldn't talk.

'You don't need to talk, Morris, just listen. I saw you last night and you saw what Richard did. And yet,' I sighed in disgust. 'And yet, you still instructed your weasels in the press to pour scorn on what we both know was the greatest Henry we have ever seen. What's wrong with you, man, have you no shame? He's just better than us, can't you accept that. He's a once in a generation talent! It's just our bad luck that it's our generation, but why not celebrate the fact that we will get to share the stage with him? History will not judge you kindly, Morris.'

I was angry, breathing heavily. Morris pulled a sheet of paper towards him and scribbled a line on it then passed it to me.

History is written by the winners!

Our conversation was over.

The next day, I was up early and popped into the theatre. It was only 9 a.m. but Morris was already in his office and his voice was back. He looked concerned.

'What's wrong?'

He looked grave. 'Beatrice just called to say that Richard has gone missing.'

'Missing? He was exhausted when I saw him yesterday, I find it hard to believe that he's gone for a walk.'

'According to Beatrice, he's been doing a lot of walking lately.'

'During the night?' I couldn't conceal my scepticism.

'Apparently, he went missing at about midnight. Beatrice went into his room to check on him and he wasn't there. At first, she thought he had just gone out for a walk, but when he hadn't returned by 4 a.m., she realised that something was wrong.'

'When did she call you?'

'Just after seven.'

'Why did she leave it so long?'

'She didn't want to bother me too early. Can you believe it?'

'Has she called the police?'

'And said what? My husband's been out all night. Hardly be counted as a missing person, would he.'

Morris had a point. I assumed the police wouldn't be interested until at least twenty-four hours had passed. There was one thing I could do.

'I'm going up to the Long Marston railway bridge. Apparently, he likes watching the trains go by.'

Morris shook his head. 'I didn't believe that he was fit enough to walk six miles but not to come to the theatre, until the other night.' He stared absentmindedly out of the window. 'Never seen the like of it. Why didn't he make himself more available?'

'Well, you haven't exactly made him welcome, have you?' The words were out of my mouth before I could stop them.

Morris looked at me reprovingly. 'He's not been well enough to be trusted with a big role. When he's better, I'll review it. Until then, he needs to prove to me he's fit to be on stage with us.'

I should have argued; the whole company knew the truth, but

what was the point? Morris had made his decision; Richard would never get a major opportunity unless he moved on. For Morris, there could be only one king and the crown lay upon his own head.

'I'm going up there, just in case he's taken himself to the bridge and forgotten to come back.'

It sounded ridiculous but, if you had seen Richard during the course of his illness, you would understand that he was capable of losing himself for hours on end.

'You want to borrow my bike? It's by the stage door.'

'Yeah, that would be helpful.'

'It's the yellow Claude Butler.'

'That's great. Thanks, Morris.'

I hadn't ridden a bike for a while and the first few yards were a nightmare, but the old saying was true, "just like riding a bike", once you've done it, you never forget. By the time I hit the back lanes behind Welford-on-Avon, I was riding like a teenager. The three speed Sturmey-Archer gear change worked beautifully and I was covering the ground quickly. I climbed over the hill at the back of Welford, which soon reminded me that I wasn't bike fit.

As I crested the top of the hill, I was rewarded with a magnificent view of the Cotswolds. From here, it was downhill into Long Marston and then a mile of flat ground to the bridge where I hoped to find Richard.

As I cruised down the hill, I was overcome with a feeling of dread. From behind me, the sound of emergency bells came speeding past and overtook me as I entered the village. It was an ambulance. Something was wrong here, very wrong. I tried to increase my pace but fear of what I might find made me slow down. I just *knew* I wasn't going to like what I found at the bridge.

I arrived about three minutes after the ambulance. My worst fears were confirmed when a policeman held up his hand to stop me approaching.

'Sorry, sir, the bridge is closed.'

'Why?' It was a stupid question; I already knew the answer.

'There's been an accident, someone has fallen onto the line.'

'Is he OK?'

'Not after the Cheltenham train hit him.'

It was typical dark British humour, but the poor constable wasn't to know that it was my friend lying on the rails.

'It's not bloody funny,' I snapped. 'That man's my friend.' I jumped off the bike and shoved it at him. As he caught it, I veered away and ran past him.

'Sir, you can't go up there.'

I ignored his calls and sprinted to the top of the bridge. A senior officer, who had been looking over the parapet, turned towards me as I approached.

'I wouldn't look over there, sir, not a pretty sight.'

'But … My friend, he's—'

'Dead, sir,' he bowed his head.

I took a deep breath and crept to the edge of the parapet; I had to know for sure. As I looked down, I saw Richard. His eyes were open but they stared past me to another place. He was wearing his red jumper. Below his ribs, it had taken on a darker hue. It took a moment to comprehend what I was seeing. Below that darker red was … nothing. His body had been literally chopped in half by the wheels of the train. I reeled back from the bridge and vomited on the road.

'I tried to warn you, sir.'

I ignored the officer as I vomited again. I crouched on my knees, waiting for the nausea to pass and then felt a gentle tap on my shoulder.

'I'm sorry, sir, did you know him well?'

I nodded and wiped my mouth. 'He was my best friend.'

It sounded pathetic; what kind of friend had I been? The secrets I had kept from him, the things I should have said, and now it was too late. The light of that amazing talent had been extinguished and I had never told him how much I loved him. Never got the chance to see his amazing acting ability reach the pinnacle it so deserved.

The dream was over; Camelot had fallen. Richard was dead and Morris reigned, unchallenged, on the throne. He was now free to rule his domain, and I would remain his courtier; imprisoned by ambition, trapped by secrets I could never share. The sun dipped behind the clouds and, for me, I don't think it ever really shone again.

The End

Acknowledgements

All Our Yesterdays may be a small book but it's got a big heart. I wanted to go back to Stratford-upon-Avon, 1932, just as the theatre was reopening after the big fire of 1926.

For this, I needed a change in style for the cover – a more *art deco* railway advert feel – and I think Amy Newport pulled it off brilliantly. Huge thanks to Amy, who you should all check out, a fabulous artist and even lovelier person. You can find Amy at *instagram.com/artbyamynewport/* and *x.com/Amynewport8*.

Big thanks to Pete Adlington, my usual cover go to. He's back on the next two books and helped out by doing all the setting out of the cover. Not only did Pete get married last year, he also had a baby daughter. The man doesn't do things by halves.

Thanks again to the wonderful Samantha Brownley, editor *extraordinaire*, who as always was full of sound advice, and to her husband, Dave Brownley, who handles all the online sales and promo.

Thanks to the wonderful Will Templeton for his excellent proofreading and setting out. As always, it looks fab. Big thanks to Laura Lees PR for lowering her standards to work with me.

And finally to the boss, the lovely Lou Lancaster. Still smiling after thirty-four years … What a girl!

Coming soon …

Read on for an extract from

Put Out The Light

the next book in **The Shakespeare Murders** series.

Chapter 1
The Coming Storm

The diary lay open on the table: Tuesday the first of August, 1972. Oliver stared at the empty page. He turned to the next page, which was also blank, every page was blank. He picked up his pen and continued to turn the pages until he reached Sunday the sixth. His pen hovered momentarily above the page and then he began to write.

Kill someone.

He sat back, read his entry and nodded his approval. Too much time had passed, vengeance is an impatient mistress. He stared at the words. As a statement it showed intent but lacked clarity. Who should he kill? He had a list of victims but who should be next? He started to write a fresh list and stopped after three. Was that all? There were so many that he could have included. He looked again at the list, every name was female; women he had loved, trusted, and all had betrayed him.

Did their betrayal warrant the death penalty he was imposing upon them?

A voice of caution sounded in his head. *O, beware, my lord of jealousy. It is the green-eyed monster which doth mock the meat it feeds on.* He recognised the quote but this was not jealousy; he cared nothing for the affections of these women.

The weeks had passed and spring had turned to summer. Peace had descended once more upon Stratford. He had waited, allowed the storm to subside, all the time thinking, planning. Allowing his mind to clear; it was time for the second act. He stood up and gazed into the mirror above the fireplace. The face that looked back at him was calm, focused … But the eyes? They blazed with intent. He raised his hands in front of him. '"Put out the light, and then put out the light."' He smiled. 'Let the play begin.'

Chapter 2
Waiting

Toby Marlowe stood in the incident room at Guild Street studying the whiteboard. The faces of the dead stared out at him. It was hard to look at those photos. He had failed to save them; failed to catch their killer. Nearly seven weeks had passed since Gerard Soames had been found beside the bandstand. Propped up in a seated position and tied back to it, held in place, looking towards the theatre. There was a message there, he knew it. All of the victims were linked to the theatre. The killer was playing with them. Four murders in just a couple of weeks and then … nothing. This was not the end, it couldn't be.

'Searching for inspiration?'

He turned. Fred Williams was standing in the entrance to the room. 'What are we missing?'

Fred shrugged. 'The killer.'

Toby looked back at the whiteboard. 'We know who that is.'

'Do we?'

'Oliver Lawrence, it has to be.' Toby tapped the photo that was fixed to the top right-hand corner of the board. 'He's our man.'

'You think he is but what proof do we have? We don't even know if he's still alive.'

Toby couldn't argue with that. Nobody had even reported seeing him in Stratford. Toby tapped the photo again. 'This is the only picture we have of him and it's nearly sixteen years old. We have no idea what he looks like now.'

Fred sighed. 'We don't. All we can do is keep looking for whoever it is—'

'It's Lawrence, I know it.'

'*You* think it,' said Fred. '*We* don't know it. He's a good candidate but we've made him fit the crimes. What if it's not him, what then?'

'It's him, I know it's him.'

Fred walked over to the kettle. 'Fancy a cuppa? Give you a chance to clear your head. You're letting this case get to you.'

Toby glanced at the faces staring out at him. Desmond and Tabitha Tharpe, Terry Fibs and Gerard Soames. All victims of the *Shakespeare Killer*. That's what the press had christened him. He was out there somewhere, waiting.

'Staring at that won't bring you any answers.'

Toby turned his back to the board and headed over to where Fred was opening the biscuit tin. 'What will?'

'The next victim.'

For a moment, Toby didn't know what to say. Fred had said it so casually.

'Are you serious? That's our plan?'

'Not our only plan but it is a plan.' Fred clicked off the kettle and began to pour. 'We can keep going over the details of each murder, checking and rechecking the evidence.' He paused for a moment and looked at Toby. 'I think we both know that's not going to bring us anything. Our murderer hasn't left any clues to his identity. He's not made a mistake.'

'He's been lucky,' hissed Toby.

'Lucky is all he needs to be. The end result is we have four victims and we don't have a clue who did it.' Toby went to protest but Fred silenced him with a raised hand. 'We have nothing tangible; we think it's Oliver Lawrence but, without any evidence, it might as well be Jack the Ripper.'

'So we just wait for him to kill again?'

'Can you come up with anything better? He's done nothing for six weeks now, maybe he's finished.'

Toby shook his head. 'You don't believe that.'

'No, I don't. He's planning, he's coming back for more. We

just have to be ready for him when he does.' Fred passed Toby a mug of tea. 'We are watching all of Sir Morris' players. At some point soon, our murderer is going to show up and that's when we catch him.'

Fred's plan was a good one, there was just one flaw in it: they hadn't considered the director who had caused so many problems with her wild ideas. If Toby and Fred could have seen Oliver's list, they would have realised nobody was watching Lizzie Birchwood.